Countdown to Halloween

Dianna Houx

Contents

-Days till Halloween-

Twenty

"Hey, Grace, what are you doing?" Molly asked as she entered the dining room. She put her keys and purse down on the far end of the table, careful not to get too close to the project Grace was working on.

Without looking up from the sign she was painting, Grace replied. "We thought it was time to officially name the B&B, so Cole made this sign for me to put up in front of the house. The only problem is, I can't come up with a name."

"Why do you think you need a name?"

Surprised to hear the marketing queen pose such a question, Grace finally looked up and raised her brow. "I thought you, of all people, would be all over me giving this place a cute name. Don't you think it would help us stand out? Or, at the very least, be easier for our guests to find?"

Molly went silent momentarily, then sighed as she pulled out a chair and sat. "You're right; we should have done this a long time ago. I am really off my game these days." She shifted uncomfortably as she struggled to fit her pregnant belly between the chair and the table. "Between the pregnancy, the new business, and the hotel, I just can't keep up anymore."

Grace reached over and patted her hand. "You're doing great!" she replied enthusiastically. "Besides, this is a group effort. You don't have to be responsible for everything."

"I suppose," she looked doubtful.

"I mean it," Grace reassured her. "Now, why don't you help me pick a name?"

"We should probably pick one for the hotel as well," she said thoughtfully. "It will be much easier to get the hotel listed on search engines if it has a name."

This was news to Grace. "I thought we agreed we wouldn't run the hotel year-round?"

"Yes, but that doesn't mean we should avoid listing it online. These days, no one's willing to trust a business that doesn't have an internet presence. It's not a big deal to blackout dates out of season and only allow people to make reservations for our open dates. In fact, it could even help us manage our bookings."

"Okay, fine. As long as this doesn't turn into another scenario like the one with Evie's wedding," Grace said, referring to last summer when Molly and Grant rented out the hotel to guests before it was ready.

Molly sighed again. "I know you're still upset about that, but think of it this way: we made enough money to replace the roof and remodel two of the three floors. Not bad for a couple of week's worth of work!"

Grace stared at Molly silently.

"Okay, I know you're still mad about the roof. Grant and I should have never agreed to buy the hotel without an inspection, but everything worked out in the end, right?" Molly asked hopefully.

The hotel and the two highly stressful weeks she spent remodeling it were still a sore subject for Grace. She had been against buying it in the first place but had gone along with it to keep the peace. Running a seasonal bed and breakfast and caring for her elderly granny already kept her busy enough; she didn't need to add a third thing to her full plate. But, and she might never admit this out loud, she was proud of her work at the hotel. Still, if they had listened to her in the first place, they could have avoided many of their problems. None of that mattered now. What's done is done, as Granny would say.

"Why don't we focus on coming up with a couple of names," Grace said, changing the subject. She loved Molly and didn't want to fight with her. Especially since she was due with her first baby any day now. The last thing Grace wanted to do was cause her friend unnecessary stress.

As if sensing the tension, or more likely, a new toy to play with, Piper jumped up on the table and began to swat at the paintbrush in Grace's hand. With a laugh, Molly grabbed the adorable black and white kitten, cuddling her to her chest as she cooed over her. "That sounds great," she smiled. "We might need some help, though; this is a big decision."

"Help with what?" Rebekah asked as she walked in the door and set her stuff down next to Molly's. "What big decision?" she looked pointedly at Grace as if expecting an announcement.

"Help with naming the B&B and hotel," Molly replied.

"Oh," Rebekah looked disappointed. "I guess I can help with that."

"Were you hoping for something else?" Grace asked innocently.

Rebekah rolled her eyes as she took a seat next to Grace. "Not that I'm not loving the change of pace from 'bustling New York' to 'so slow you could get passed by a snail Winterwood,' it's just we need some excitement around here."

"You mean a wedding," Grace deadpanned.

"I would settle for a big party if it would help pay the bills. Small towns are great, but it's hard to earn a living when you don't have paying customers."

"I thought you were advertising in the surrounding cities?" asked Molly.

"That's the plan, but I was holding off until the hotel was ready. Hard to entice people to come here when there's nowhere for them to stay," she blew out a breath. "Anyway, let's figure out those names. I'm assuming this is the last hurdle we need to jump before the hotel opens for business?" she asked hopefully.

Grace was about to respond when a popular country song began to play, startling them all. Rebekah quickly grabbed her phone and looked at the number on the screen. "It's an unknown number," she said out loud. "Probably spam."

"You better answer anyway. All of your potential customers will be unknown numbers," Molly explained.

"Good point," Rebekah swiped at the screen. "Hello, this is Rebekah Rutherford."

Molly and Grace sat silently as they eavesdropped on Rebekah's side of the conversation, not that they got much out of the "uh-huh and sounds goods."

As soon as Rebekah hung up, Molly's phone rang, and she repeated the process almost to the tee.

Grace and Rebekah were fidgeting in their seats by the time she hung up, though for different reasons. "One of you want to tell me what's going on!" Grace exclaimed.

Rebekah and Molly looked at each other with huge grins on their faces. "Go ahead," Molly nodded toward Rebekah.

"That was the radio station," Rebekah began, excitement dripping from her voice. "They're doing a huge promotion for Halloween, and they want me to run it!"

"That's great!" Grace said, a bit bewildered. "So, you're going to do some kind of party?" She looked at Molly. "What does this have to with you?"

"No, silly," Rebekah interrupted. "They're doing a Halloween-themed wedding! This is going to be the most fun I've ever had!"

Molly smiled gently at Grace's confusion. "They want the hotel to host the family members of the lucky bride and groom," Molly explained. "Same setup as Evie's wedding."

Another last-minute wedding? What happened to brides spending years planning their special days? Or giving guests more than a week's notice? But what did she know? She was just an innkeeper. "Guess this means we don't have to worry about booking guests for Halloween. How exactly does this help the radio station?"

"The promotion will garner a lot of attention, which will increase the amount of people tuning in, which, in turn, will increase the amount of money they can charge for advertising," Molly explained.

"Are we going to get paid for this? Or is it one of those 'donate for exposure' things?" asked Grace.

Molly made a face. "We were asked to give a discount, but it was only ten percent. Given the amount we'll save on advertising fees, it seemed a fair trade."

"What about you," Grace asked Rebekah.

"I don't know yet. I have a meeting with the producer tomorrow morning."

Things still weren't adding up for Grace. "How do they even know about us? I mean, we're an hour outside of the city. We're not exactly on their radar."

"Kenzie from the winery recommended us. The wedding is going to be held there," Rebekah replied.

That actually made sense. "Guess that means it's time to get to work," Grace sighed. "We only have twenty days until Halloween..." she trailed off as a thought popped into her head. "You know, we should bring back the fair. Those usually last around three days, and that would give the guests something to do while they're waiting around for the wedding."

"A fair sounds fun," Rebekah shrugged. "Not exactly a wedding or a party, but I would be willing to help."

"I was thinking we would do some kind of haunted hotel event at the hotel," Molly chimed in. "Maybe charge a small fee to bring in a little extra revenue?"

Undoubtedly, Grace would be in charge of bringing that little idea to life. For once, she had a project she could look forward to. She had always loved Halloween but had never had the money to celebrate it. This year was going to be different. This year, she had an excellent excuse for going all-out and putting together the best Halloween experience this town had ever seen. It might not make up for all the years she missed out on as a kid, but it would come close.

"Sounds good to me," Grace replied. "We still need those names, though. It would be nice to have them ready for the radio station when they start advertising."

"Why don't we all give it some thought, make a list of names, and then meet back here tomorrow to discuss them," said Molly. She struggled to get to her feet but ultimately managed, with a bit of help from Grace, to get out of her chair. "I need to return to the office and create a promotion package. I'll see you guys later."

Grace watched her go, then turned to Rebekah. "Does she seem okay to you?"

"Pregnancy stress," Rebekah replied as she dug through her purse. She pulled out a notebook and pen and saw Grace watching her. "It's almost time for the baby to come, right?"

Grace nodded. "Isn't that a good thing?"

"I'm not exactly an expert, but Molly's life will change dramatically once
the baby's here. She'll have to make some changes career-wise, and I think that's getting to her."

"Seems kind of unfair," Grace mused.

Rebekah shrugged. "Life is unfair. She wanted the kid, so sacrifices must be made."

"You sound a little bitter," Grace observed.

She focused on her notebook, studiously avoiding Grace's gaze to hide her anger. "I spent the first part of my life as an accessory for my socialite mom and the last part as a bartering tool for my dad. At no point did either of them consider the fact they chose to bring an actual human into the world. A human with her own wants, needs, and dreams for the future. I believe Molly and Grant will be great parents, but at some point, they will have to learn to put their baby first and their careers second."

Rebekah's words sounded harsh, but Grace supposed she had a point. Molly and Grant almost divorced by allowing their careers to rule their lives. Moving to Winterwood was supposed to be their chance to slow down and start over, yet it took less than a month for them to start new businesses and fall back into their old habits of working seven days a week. This baby may be the thing that finally helps them change their priorities once and for all.

-Days till Halloween-

Nineteen

Grace wasn't kidding when she said she was looking forward to Halloween. She'd been preparing for months, watching every diy Halloween decoration video she could find online. Yes, she could probably afford to go to one of the pop-up Halloween stores and buy what she wanted, but since she was decorating the house and the hotel, that would be a lot of money and old habits die-hard. Besides, making her own was so much fun!

Every video she watched used items from the dollar store. Since she knew she would need a lot of items and didn't want to buy out the stores and prevent others from having fun, too, she had placed bulk orders ahead of time. Last night, Cole had driven her to the city in his truck and helped her pick up all her goodies. It had been far more romantic than it sounds, the trip reminding them both of when they had first worked together last Valentine's Day. Honestly, it was hard to believe they'd only been dating around eight months. In some ways, it felt like they'd known each other forever; in other ways, it felt like barely any time had passed.

Now that things were winding up on the farm, they would have much more time to spend together, and Grace couldn't wait. Starting with today. Cole was due to arrive in a couple of hours with some hay she planned to decorate on the front lawn. She'd seen some videos for that, too, most people using paint to create characters out of the large, round bales. Since this was a family-friendly B&B, she had to be careful not to make anything too scary. She wanted this to be a safe place, not one that scared the children.

Speaking of children, if they were going to do a haunted hotel, she would have to find a way to strike the right balance of scary and fun. Not an easy feat to achieve when you have precisely zero experience, but, as with everything else, she was sure she could find a video or two that would, at the very least, give her some ideas. Since the first two floors would be rented out to guests for the wedding, that left the third floor and the basement as possible locations.

In its current condition, the basement looked like something out of a horror movie. Which was convenient if that was the aesthetic she was going for, but it would likely require a liability waiver from everyone who entered. Since actual terror was not her goal, this left the third floor. Now that the roof was fixed, it was safe to go up there again, though the rooms still needed extensive remodeling, which could be used to her advantage. She'd have to give this some more thought.

"What on earth happened in here?" Molly exclaimed as she entered the dining room. "It looks like a Halloween store threw up in here!"

Rebekah, who had followed Molly into the room, appeared startled by the chaos. "What are you doing?" she asked, her eyes wide.

"Living my best life," Grace deadpanned in response.

At that moment, Piper, who had been gleefully batting some of the smaller, hollow pumpkins around the room, ran over to Rebekah and dropped a plastic spider at her feet. Not realizing it was fake, Rebekah jumped back with a scream, causing poor Piper to run away and hide under a nearby chair.

Grace laughed and bent down to retrieve the spider. "It's just a decoration," she reassured the poor woman.

"I realize you have two places to decorate, but this seems a little extreme," Rebekah waved to indicate the decorations strewn all over the room. "Are these for the town as well?" she asked hopefully.

"Nope," Grace shook her head. "These are all for the house." She beamed at them, then went back to organizing her supplies. Spiders in one pile, pumpkins in another, Halloween-themed gnomes in yet another. By the time she was done, every spot in the house, inside and out, would sport a decoration. It will be glorious!

"You are way too happy," Molly said suspiciously. "Did something happen we need to know about?"

Grace rolled her eyes. "Honestly, guys, I'm just excited for Halloween. I've always loved the holiday, but we never had the money to celebrate. All throughout elementary school, Granny would make costumes for me to wear to the classroom party, but I was never allowed to trick-or-treat like the other kids. This is the first year I can go all-out, so I intend to do so."

"Aww, why weren't you allowed to trick-or-treat?" asked Molly.

"Because we didn't have money for Halloween candy. Granny said it wasn't polite to take if we couldn't afford to give in return, so we stayed home and watched movies with the porch light off each year. It was very sad and very embarrassing. The kids at school made fun of me for weeks after. For that and my costumes..." she trailed off as she picked up a black cat and studied it. The memories still stung even though decades had passed.

"What was wrong with your costumes?" asked Rebekah. Her nose was scrunched up, confusion apparent on her face.

Grace sighed. "We couldn't afford costumes either, so every year, Granny would make my costume. One year, she painted a cardboard box to look like a juice box with a pool noodle sticking out of the top for the straw. Another year, she had me wear a laundry basket with clothes draped around me to look like a dirty clothes basket. The last year, I wore my Christmas dress with cardboard wings and went as an angel."

"Those sound adorable!" exclaimed Molly.

"And original," said Rebekah. "That kind of thing would go viral on social media today."

"Oh sure, these days, influencer moms would be lauded as heroes, and their little darlings would be the most popular in the class. Those days, I was the poor kid who stuck out like a sore thumb amongst a sea of store-bought costumes." She put down the cat and looked up to see the sadness on their faces. "It's okay," she smiled. "That's all behind me now, and I'm looking forward to making up for lost time."

"Well, I, for one, am happy to help you," Rebekah said with a smile.

"I am, too," said Molly. She pulled out a chair and sat down, squealing and jumping back up as she pulled out a handful of colored lights.

"Hey, you found my lights! I was wondering where they went," said Grace.

Molly made a show of checking her chair and the surrounding area before she sat back down. "Your lights almost gave me a heart attack," she deadpanned.

"I'm sorry," Grace replied sheepishly. "I guess it is kind of a mess in here. I'll try to have things organized by dinner."

"It's fine," she said dismissively. "Anyway, are you two ready to discuss names for the hotel and b&b?"

Grace and Rebekah each took a seat, carefully checking for stray decorations before they sat down. "Oh, I almost forgot," Grace popped back up and ran over to the counter in the kitchen, carefully carrying back a tray she set down on the table in front of them. "My latest recipe," she announced with a flourish.

"Ooh, do I smell pumpkin bread?" Gladys asked from the doorway. She shuffled over to the table, Granny close behind.

As the ladies took their seats, Grace served the bread. She had labored for hours over this recipe. She usually wasn't one to follow trends, but she loved pumpkins and had been looking forward to all things pumpkin spice.

"This is amazing!" Molly exclaimed. "I'm pretty sure I've died and gone to heaven!"

"It's the candied pecans," Grace nodded. "They really make the bread."

They ate silently for a while, everyone engrossed in their new favorite snack. When the last crumb had been consumed, Molly cleared her throat. "We really need to come up with those names, ladies. The radio station has already begun airing their promos, so the clock is ticking."

"How about the Hotel of Winterwood?" asked Grace. "It's simple and to the point."

Rebekah crinkled her nose. "No offense, but we need something a little jazzier." She appeared to give it some thought. "How about something like the Cozy Inn or the Cozy Hotel?"

"That's cute!" said Granny.

"I agree," said Gladys. "For me, it conjures up images of fireplaces and hot cocoa, which is great for about half the year. Would that work for the hot season?"

"I'm not sure," said Molly. "I think we're going in the right direction, but since we're only open for holidays and special events, we need to play to that."

"How about the Holiday House, only something spicier like Holidaze?" suggested Grace.

"It's interesting," said Rebekah. "I think we definitely need 'holiday' in the name. How about the Enchanted Holiday Inn?"

Granny picked at the napkin in front of her. "How about the Enchanted Holiday Hideaway? This seems to be where people come to get away from things..." She looked pointedly at Molly and Rebekah.

"I love that," Rebekah smiled. "Plus, we're in the middle of nowhere, which makes it very fitting in that aspect as well."

"Considering all the people Grace has helped, the Enchanted part is also fitting," mused Molly. "It gives this place a magical feel," she nodded as she worked through it. "Yes, Enchanted Holiday Hideaway is perfect." She grabbed her phone from her purse and typed the name into her notes. "One down, one to go!"

"Should we give the hotel a 'normal' sounding name or something cute and catchy?" asked Grace. "We don't want to confuse people."

"No, we don't want to do that, but we do want to stand out from the crowd. This is not a hotel people can visit in the middle of the night. That needs to be clear, not that we'd get much of that anyway," said Molly.

"Let's see, there's Spruce Inn, Holly Berry Inn, or Cedar Lodge if you want to go with a nature theme," said Gladys.

"Or Liberty Inn, or even Trails End," said Granny.

"Trails End sounds a little ominous!" Grace laughed. "It would be perfect for Halloween!"

Rebekah looked up from her own notebook. "Ooh, you should use

that as part of the Haunted Hotel," she told Grace. "I don't know how, but I'm sure you'll figure it out."

"Gee, thanks!" Grace rolled her eyes as she laughed. "Although...you may be on to something."

"What about Inspiration's Rest? That plays to the Enchanted theme," said Rebekah.

Unable to sit still any longer, Grace began to clear the table. "That would make a great name for a writer's retreat. You should write that down in case we ever decide to host one."

Granny stopped shredding her napkin and began to wipe up the mess she'd made. "Winter Resort?" she threw out. "Never mind, that makes us sound like a ski lodge, doesn't it?"

"Well, we do live in Winterwood. I don't think having Winter in the title is completely out of the question," Molly said thoughtfully. "What about Winter Haven? I think that goes pretty well with Hideaway."

"Winter Haven, what?" asked Grace. "Resort? Retreat? Inn and Spa?"

"Retreat," said Rebekah. "Winter Haven Retreat. It pairs perfectly with Enchanted Holiday Hideaway. It will give guests the feeling that they're going someplace special. Someplace they can escape their daily lives and just relax."

"Do you mind if I use that last part?" asked Molly. "It will make a great marketing slogan."

Rebekah beamed at her. "Not at all."

Molly looked around the table. "So, do we all agree on Enchanted Holiday Hideaway and Winter Haven Retreat?" Each lady nodded enthusiastically as she looked around the table one by one. "Great! Thanks, everyone, that took far less time than expected."

Granny looked around the room, her eyes widening at the sight. "Grace, um," she began.

Grace held up her hand. "I know, Granny; I promise it will all be cleaned up by dinner time."

A hopeful look crossed Grany's face. "Is it time to bust out the old sewing machine again?"

"What do you mean?" asked Grace.

"Don't you remember all those costumes I made you when you were a kid?"

Boy, did she. Grace had done her best to hide her true feelings from Granny when she was a kid. Even then, she knew it wasn't Granny's fault they didn't have the money for things like that. "Of course, Granny. What about them?"

"I had so much fun making those for you; I was just thinking how nice it would be to do it again."

Grace's heart melted at the look on Granny's face. It was clear for all to see how special those memories were for Granny. And here Grace had been, lamenting how 'awful' that experience had been for her. What a selfish, spoiled brat she had been. "I would love for you to make a costume for me, Granny," Grace wrapped her arm around Granny's waist and laid her head on her shoulder so she couldn't see the shame on her face.

"Wonderful!" Granny exclaimed. "I believe the sewing machine was moved to the attic. If you could be a dear and bring it down for me, I'll get started immediately!"

Gladys looked at Rebekah and Molly. "Either of you want a costume? Might as well join in the fun!"

"Me!" Rebekah and Molly said in unison. "Although this little guy or gal might complicate things a bit," Molly laughed as she pointed to her bulging stomach.

"Nonsense," Gladys waved her hand dismissively. "I'll just make sure I make something long and flowing. Now, we'll work on ideas while you girls finish here. Oh, and we'll need you to come by for measurements sometime in the next few days."

Grace stepped back and smiled as she watched Granny and Gladys shuffle off toward Granny's room. They were chattering like school girls excited about the upcoming dance. It had been a while since Grace had seen them so excited, the sight warming her heart. This was going to be the best Halloween ever!

-Days till Halloween-

Eighteen

Grace had been kidding herself when she claimed she would have the house decorated by dinner the night before. Not only did she still have to make a lot of the decorations, it took a lot of time and a lot of going up and down ladders to hang decorations from every corner of the house. Thankfully, Cole had come over, as promised, and helped her complete quite a bit of it. The rest she had piled to the side for another day.

Cole's hay bales were sitting on the lawn, waiting patiently to be turned into something spooky. Grace had seen a cute skeleton band in one of the box stores the other day and was trying to figure out how to turn huge piles of hay into something similar. The plan was to hang enough string lights outside so passersby could see the decorations without the need for floodlights. She would hide speakers around the house and hook them up to play her Halloween playlist. Toss up some fake spiderwebs and plastic skeletons, and she would be done.

The hotel would be a little different. People tended to have different expectations when it came to places like that. There, she would need the right blend of decorated and clean. So, she was thinking themed floral arrangements, themed soaps, and maybe a few skeletons propped up in chairs throughout the lobby and dining room. The real excitement would occur in the 'haunted' part on the third floor, though she still wasn't entirely sure how that would work.

Rebekah's suggestion of using 'trail's end' for inspiration was working. At one point, Winterwood was a booming railroad town. It was where cattle ranchers from both sides of the state drove their cattle to be loaded onto train cars and ferried off to other states. Maybe the hotel could be haunted by ranchers who never left? It would have been the 'end of the trail' for them, that's for sure. But what would be their motivation to haunt the hotel? Were they murdered by money-hungry thieves? Or by cattle rustlers? She'd have to give it some more thought. Cole may have some ideas.

Speaking of Cole, she spotted his black cowboy hat and knew he was walking toward the barn, where she was again mucking out the horse stalls. The closer he got, the more intense the butterflies fluttering in her stomach became. After eight months of dating, she still felt those familiar feelings. Would it always be that way? She certainly hoped so. She couldn't imagine a day she didn't love him with every fiber of her being.

"Hey, handsome," she greeted him, reaching up on her tippy-toes to kiss him.

"Hey, beautiful," he replied, eagerly returning her kiss. "What's on the agenda for the day?" he asked as they reluctantly broke apart.

"More decorating," she sighed happily.

Cole grinned at her enthusiasm. "It's nice to see you this excited about one of your upcoming events. Usually, you're just stressed out."

"It's nice to be excited," she laughed. "Although," she said flirtatiously. "A certain cowboy may have something to do with that excitement," she batted her eyelashes at him.

"Is that so?" he leaned down and kissed her again, pulling her up against him.

The sound of a woman screaming interrupted their passionate embrace. "What the heck?" Cole said, a confused look on his face. "Who was that?"

They looked around for the source of the scream, but no one appeared to be there. "Should we check the field?" Grace asked. She was just as confused as he was.

Cole took her hand and cautiously led her out of the barn. The sight that greeted them caused them both to stop in their tracks. There, on the side of the pen he kept his bull in, was Shelley, perched on the top rung of the fence, phone in hand as she did...who knows what.

Without a word, Cole dropped Grace's hand and ran just as Shelley lost her balance and fell face-first into the pen. Into the pen with the bull. The bull who was not amused to find a strange woman invading his territory.

As the bull began to charge, Shelley began to scream in earnest as she lay frozen in fear on the ground. The hooves were in the air, poised to land directly on her as Cole reached under the fence, grabbed her legs, and dragged her over to his side.

"Oh my gosh, Shelley, are you okay?" asked Grace. Her heart was racing out of control as she watched the bull stomp and snort in disgust. Shelley would be a goner if Cole hadn't gotten there in time.

"Did either of you get that on film?" she asked from her position on the ground.

Grace stared at her in stunned silence. The woman had clearly gone mad. Her entire body was shaking in fear, yet that was her concern? "Um, no?" Grace finally replied.

"What are you doing here?" Cole asked through gritted teeth. "Do you have any idea how much danger you were in? If I hadn't pulled you out of there in time, that bull would have killed you."

Shelley slowly sat up and ran her fingers through her hair. "But you did, so it's all good, right?"

"No, Shelley, it is not 'all good.' What is with these unhinged women thinking they have the right to trespass on my property?" he mumbled. Cole took off his hat and ran his hand through his hair.

Grace had seen that look before; he was scared. Shelley's stunt had clearly rattled him, and while she might not be taking it seriously, he definitely was. Grace took a closer look at Shelley. "Why are you wearing a wedding dress?"

"It's part of my gimmick, duh," she rolled her eyes as if that was something everyone should know.

Cole raised a brow. "Your gimmick? What in the world are you talking about?"

A look of disgust crossed Shelley's face. "You two are way too young to be this clueless," she snarked.

"Shelley," Cole prodded, the warning in his voice unmistakable.

"Whatever," she rolled her eyes. "Since you old fogies are clearly living in the last century, let me help you. Someone posted a video of me catching the bouquet at Evie's wedding, which went viral. Since I'm not one to let an opportunity pass me by, I've been capitalizing on that fame ever since. I have almost ten thousand followers," she said proudly.

"Okay," Cole drawled. "What does that have to do with my ranch? More specifically, with my bullpen?"

"I was trying to get the bull to come to me so I could jump on his back and ride him. I had a bet with my fans that I could stay on for longer than eight seconds."

"Are you insane?" Cole roared. "That bull weighs over two thousand pounds; he could have killed you!"

"People ride bulls all the time," she huffed.

"No, people ride mechanical bulls. No one, and I repeat, no one, goes around trying to ride real bulls. Especially ones they don't know and don't own," he gritted out. His jaw was clenched, as were his hands. Shelley had crossed a line but still couldn't grasp the severity of the situation.

"People in the rodeo do it all the time," she spat back.

"When did you become a professional bull rider?" he asked sarcastically. "Please don't answer that," he interrupted before she could speak. "How about this? Why aren't you trying to get yourself killed at your parent's ranch?"

"They kicked me out," she shrugged.

"Really?" Grace asked, surprised by the woman's admission. Shelley had always been the golden child, her parents standing by her even when she did the most despicable things to her sister.

"It's all Evie's fault," Shelley whined.

Grace rolled her eyes at the too-familiar words. According to Shelley, any time she didn't get her way, which was rare, it was her sister's fault. "I highly doubt that."

Shelley crossed her arms over her chest and stuck out her tongue. "I don't care what you think; it's the truth. Evie seriously embarrassed them by not inviting them to her wedding. The whole town turned against my family, and now they're blaming me even though it's obviously her fault."

Grace opened her mouth to defend her friend, but Cole held up his hand to silence her. "I don't care," he ground out. "You need to find somewhere else to pull your stunts," he told Shelley. "I better not ever catch you here again."

"Or what?" she asked snottily.

"Or next time, I'll leave you to face the consequences of your actions."

Shelley looked at the bull and then back at Cole, a look of horror crossing her face. "You wouldn't," she whispered.

Cole stepped toward her, bending down so they were eye level. "Yes, I would," he said menacingly.

All color drained from her face, leaving her white as a ghost. She stepped back, her shaking legs causing her to wobble a bit. "Fine," she muttered. "I'll never come here again."

Grace had to stifle a laugh at her tone. She sounded like a haughty customer threatening to never shop at a store again. The whole thing would have been comical if not for the genuine threat to her life.

"Do you think she believed me?" Cole asked.

"Yeah, I'm pretty sure she believed you. Don't be surprised if word gets around that you threatened to turn her into bull feed."

Cole wrapped his arms around Grace's waist and pulled her close. "If there is anyone left in town who actually believes that, then they're as big a fool as she is."

"I know, baby," Grace said soothingly. She ran her hands up and down his back as she attempted to help calm his racing heart. "Are you okay?" she asked quietly.

He didn't answer right away; he just stood there holding her. "Yeah," he finally said. "It's just, what if I hadn't been there to save her?" He shook his head as images flashed through his mind.

"But you were there," Grace said reassuringly. She hugged him tighter as if she could squeeze the images from his mind. "I just hope you don't have to pay a price for doing it."

"I only said what I did so she would be too scared to come here again. Shelley has never had to face consequences in her life. Threats would not have worked; they would have only encouraged her."

"You're probably right. Although, she did say her parents kicked her out. Maybe she'll finally get her act together?" Grace said hopefully. "She does have a baby now."

"Oh yeah, and where was that baby while she was out here acting a fool?"

"Good point," Grace conceded. "Well, she's going to have to do something now that she's been cut off."

"Who said she's been cut off? All she said was her parents kicked her out, and they only did that to save face. I wouldn't be surprised to learn they're still paying her way."

"Fair enough," Grace conceded a second time. "How about we do something to take our minds off this?" she asked. "All this stress is bad for your health."

"What do you have in mind?" he asked, his brow raised.

"Well, I did just spend the morning cleaning up after your horses..." she smiled mischievously.

"Hmm, I think I could help you out," he grinned as he pulled her in for another kiss. Hopefully, there will be no more interruptions.

-Days till Halloween-

Seventeen

Grace was setting the breakfast table when Molly and Rebekah walked in. "Hey," Grace greeted them. "Do you two know anything about Shelley's new social media fame?"

Molly snorted. "I suppose that's one way of putting it."

"What do you mean?" Grace asked.

"The video of Shelley crashing the bouquet toss went viral. Ever since, she's been doing more and more ridiculous stunts to maintain her fame."

"Is it working?"

Molly looked at Rebekah. "What do you think?"

Rebekah shook her head. "Those kinds of things tend to work for a while but are not sustainable. Eventually, she will either run out of ideas or seriously hurt herself. For what it's worth, my money's on the latter."

"I agree," Molly nodded. "She's already struggling to maintain her numbers. It's tough to keep people's attention these days. Why do you ask?"

"She was almost trampled by a bull yesterday," Grace explained. "The first thing she asked after Cole saved her was if we got it on video." Grace shuddered at the memory.

"That's terrible," Rebekah said sympathetically. "Cole must have been so upset."

"You have no idea," Grace agreed. "He had to scare her pretty badly to ensure she didn't return and try again."

"Poor Cole," Molly shook her head. "I'm starting to think he may need security out there!" she joked.

"I'm starting to think he'd agree," Grace quipped. "Between Shelley and Valerie, he's had his hands full with unwanted guests."

"Speaking of Valerie, what happened to her?" asked Rebekah.

Grace began setting hot plates of food on the counter, buffet-style. "Last I heard, she was working on a Christmas tree farm in some little town south of here," she replied.

"That must feel like torture to her," Rebekah joked. She grabbed two plates and began to fill them with food.

"Someone's hungry today," Molly raised a brow. "I thought I was the only one eating for two!"

"Very funny," Rebekah rolled her eyes. "Thorne is on his way. You don't mind, do you, Grace? I should have asked first..."

She smiled at the thought of her friend's relationship with the new vet. "Of course, I don't mind. You know he's always welcome here."

"Thanks," she said softly.

Molly grabbed her own plate and began to fill it. "Looks like things are getting serious, eh?" she teased Rebekah. She bent over abruptly, dropping the plates on the floor as she grabbed her stomach.

Grace and Rebekah rushed to her side. "Molly, are you okay?" Grace asked as she helped her to a chair.

"I think my water just broke," Molly choked out between gasps.

Rebekah looked at Grace helplessly. "What do we do?"

"You call an ambulance while I call Grant."

Molly grabbed Grace's hand and squeezed it so tightly that Grace was sure it would break. "Hurry, please. I think she's coming."

Thorne came in, took one look at Molly, and rushed to her side. "How far apart are your contractions?" he asked.

"I-I don't know," she gasped, squeezing Grace's hand again. "It happened so fast—"

"If her hand squeezes are any indication, I'd say about a minute apart," Grace told him.

Grant, Gladys, and Granny came rushing into the kitchen simultaneously. "Molly," Grant rushed to her side, gently moving Grace out of his way. "We need to get her to the hospital," he said out loud.

"The ambulance is on the way," Rebekah reassured him.

"We don't have time to wait for them," he said, panicking. "Look at her; she could have the baby any moment."

Thorne put his hand on Grant's shoulder and squeezed. "She'll be much better off having the baby in the back of an ambulance than the back of your car if it comes to that," he said reassuringly.

"Fine," Grant relented. "But, you're a doctor, do something."

Sirens sounded before he could respond. "There, see, everything is going to be fine. I'll just go let them in."

Grant tried to help Molly to her feet, but she quickly sat back down as she was hit by another contraction. The paramedics rushed in, followed by Thorne angrily talking to one of them in a hushed voice.

The first paramedic took one look at Molly and shouted to his partner. "We're gonna need the stretcher."

"Yeah, that's what I said," Thorne rolled his eyes. The man stopped to say something, but Thorne was having none of it. "Stop wasting time and do your job." He shook his head as he watched the two rush back out of the house. "They have no respect for veterinarians," he explained to the questioning look on everyone's face.

Five minutes later, Molly was off to the hospital, Grant following close behind. "Thank you for your help," Grace said to Thorne.

"Sorry I couldn't do more," he replied. "I won't be surprised if you get a call within the hour. That baby was coming fast."

"Is that your professional opinion?" Rebekah teased.

"Yes," he deadpanned. "We should eat," he announced to the room. "There's not much we can do until they're ready for visitors."

They filled their plates and then sat at the table. "Anyone want to bet on the gender?" asked Gladys.

Obviously, she was worried about Molly and was doing her best to distract herself and likely everyone else. In the ten months Molly and Grant lived with Gladys, they'd become a close family. Gladys a surrogate mother to them both and now a surrogate grandma to the new baby.

"I heard her say 'girl,'" said Grace. "So my money is on a girl."

"Do you think she found out the gender after all?" asked Rebekah. "I thought they wanted to be surprised?"

"Mother's intuition," said Granny. "Sonograms weren't commonplace in my day, but I knew I was having a boy. I was so sure I would have bet this house."

"If that's the case, I vote girl as well," said Rebekah.

They had finished eating, cleared the table, and got ready to play a game when Grace's phone rang. "It's Grant," Grace announced to the group. She answered the phone and placed it on speaker so everyone could hear. "Hey, Grant, how is everyone?" she asked.

"Mama and baby are doing fine," he said. His tone held a mixture of relief and awe. "We know you're dying to see the new baby, but would you mind coming this afternoon? Molly is resting and—"

"Say no more," said Gladys. "There will be plenty of time for that later. Grace can stop by with Molly's things; the rest of us can wait until you're home."

"Thank you, Gladys," he said. The sound of a baby crying came over the speaker. "I need to go, Grace; the bag is by the door."

The phone went silent as they all stared at it. "He never said if it was a boy or girl," said Grace absentmindedly.

"Guess it will be your job to find out and report back to us," said Rebekah. "Make sure you take lots of pictures."

"Don't forget to get the name," said Granny.

"You should take them some food," said Gladys. "Hospital food is notoriously gross."

"Guys," Grace laughed as she held up her hand. "I've got this," she promised them. "Let's get back to the game. I have a feeling time will crawl by at a snail's pace."

***

At Gladys's suggestion, Grace waited until after dinner to visit Molly, Grant, and the new baby. It had been hard since she was dying to see them, but in the end, she knew Gladys was right about them needing time to themselves. When she reached the door to Molly's hospital room, she knocked as quietly as possible, just in case they were sleeping.

When Grant opened the door and motioned her inside, she stopped at the sight of her friend cradling her new baby. Grace had always assumed that new-mom glow was a myth, but she had been wrong. Molly had never looked happier and more at peace than she did now.

Not wanting to wake the sleeping baby, Grace waved, careful not to make a sound. Molly laughed and waved her closer. "Come meet your goddaughter," she said.

"So it is a girl!" Grace exclaimed in an excited whisper.

"Yep, Grace, meet Elizabeth Grace Hawthorne, Eliza for short," said Molly, a huge smile on her face.

Tears immediately sprung to her eyes as she looked at the baby's adorable chubby cheeks. "You named her after me?" she asked softly.

"We named her after the three most important women in our lives," said Molly. "Elizabeth for Gladys and Granny since they both share that as a middle name, and obviously, Grace for you. Without you, Grace, none of us would be here now."

"I'm sure that's not true," Grace began.

"And I'm sure it is," Molly said, cutting her off. "Last Christmas, Grant and I were on the verge of a divorce.

We're here with our beautiful new daughter, thanks to you, Granny, and Gladys."

Grant wrapped his arm around Grace's shoulder. "Thank you," he said, but his eyes were on his wife and child.

Grace wiped her eyes with the back of her hand and pulled out her phone. "If you don't mind, I promised I would bring back a picture. They might not let me back inside if I don't provide one!"

"I bet a certain cowboy would be happy to put you up for the night," Grant teased.

"Does that mean no pictures?" asked Grace. "Because the cowboy wants to see one as well. I may end up out in the barn," she joked.

"Of course, you can take a picture," said Molly. "We don't want to be responsible for that, although I should remind you there is an entire hotel full of rooms at your disposal should the need ever arise."

"Oh yeah, I forgot about that," said Grace. "Some hotel owner I am!"

Not wanting to overstay her welcome, Grace took her pictures, served the meal she had brought them, and quietly showed herself out. When she got home, she discovered her friends and family waiting for her in the dining room. "Wow, guys, news spread fast," she joked.

"Well," said Gladys. "How are they?"

"They're all doing well. The baby is a girl," Grace smiled. "And her name is Elizabeth Grace, Eliza for short."

Granny and Gladys gasped, their hands going to their hearts in unison. "They named the baby after us?"

Grace nodded as tears sprung to her eyes again. Unable to speak without her voice shaking, she pulled out her phone and opened the gallery to show them the pictures. Then she stood to the side and watched as the phone passed around the room, the group taking turns cooing over the sweet baby pictures.

"You okay?" asked Cole. He wrapped her up in a bear hug as he kissed the top of her head.

"Yeah, it's just been an emotional day."

"I can imagine," he replied. "I can stay tonight if you want me to?"

"Of course I want you to. I always want you to," she whispered.

Cole chuckled against the side of her head. "I guess it's settled then."

The phone finally returned to Grace, so she took it and showed the pictures to Cole. "She's beautiful, isn't she," she stated.

"Yes, she is," he agreed. "Some day, I hope that's you holding our daughter."

She looked up at him in surprise. "Really?"

Cole glanced around the room, then, seeing that everyone else was too busy chatting to notice them, quietly walked them out of the room and into the foyer. "Have I really done that poor of a job showing you how I feel about you?" he asked.

Grace opened her mouth to respond, then closed it again. In their eight months together, Cole had never made her question his feelings. The few times she had were because of her own insecurities, not because of anything he had done or not done. Her surprised reaction to his declaration had not been fair. "I'm sorry," she finally said. "I don't know why I was surprised. It's just we've never talked about kids. Or anything other than having more time to spend together after the growing season."

"Do you not want kids?" he asked, his tone neutral.

That was the real question, wasn't it? Did she want kids? After losing her parents at such a young age, she vowed to never put a child at risk like that. But, standing here with the love of her life, that seemed almost silly. "I know I want you," she whispered.

"That's enough for now," he said. "But I think we need to work through your feelings at some point. If you truly don't want kids, I will accept that, but if it's fear talking..."

He knew her so well. One more reason to add to the list of why she loved him. "Do you think they'll notice if we don't go back in there?" she asked.

"I'm not sure I care," he shrugged. "If you need to be alone, then you need to be alone."

Grace took his hand and led him upstairs. "What I need is to be alone with you."

Once they were safely inside her locked bedroom door, she finally let the tears she'd been holding back flow. When Cole pulled her onto the bed and into his arms, she went willingly, grateful for his support and understanding. Yes, he really did know her well.

-Days till Halloween-

Sixteen

"Molly and the baby are coming home today," Grace announced during breakfast.

"Already?" asked Rebekah. "It's barely been twenty-four hours."

"I said the same thing," Grace shrugged. "But the doctor claimed they're both doing so well he didn't see a reason to keep them any longer. I promised Molly I would go to the house and make sure everything was ready before they returned."

"I can help with that," said Rebekah.

Grace nodded and smiled at her friend. It was hard to believe she was the same entitled, spoiled, demanding woman who stayed at the B&B last February. Although, maybe this had been the real Rebekah all along. Given their history, she wouldn't be surprised if that were the case. Regardless, Grace was thankful to have her in her life.

After breakfast, they headed next door to Gladys's to prepare for Molly's return.

"What should we do first?" asked Rebekah.

"Um, check the baby's room?" suggested Grace. "I don't want to intrude, but I thought we could make sure the crib has fresh sheets, plenty of diapers and wipes, things like that."

"What about food?"

"What about it?" asked Grace. "As you already know, they usually just eat with us."

Rebekah shrugged. "That was before they had a new baby. Plus, Molly is going to need time to recover from the birth. Don't you think it will be a bit much for them to pack up the new baby and go next door every time they're hungry?"

She hadn't thought about that. Then again, what did she know about having a baby? Apparently, not that much. "So, what do you suggest?"

"Fill the fridge with snacks and easy-to-heat and serve meals. After all, you won't have time to run over here at every meal either."

"Good point. When we're done here, I'll head to the store to see what I can come up with. This may have to be an ongoing process due to the short notice," Grace replied.

Once they were convinced the house was ready for little Eliza's homecoming, they returned to the B&B to prepare food. Grace was surprised by the feelings that task brought up. She had always assumed the new baby would just slide into their lives; she never considered the possibility that their lives would dramatically change instead.

If she thought about it, and she tried not to, change was inevitable. Some day, Rebekah would get married and move out. Whether that was to Thorne or someone else was yet to be seen, but she had never hidden the fact she would like her own family. The same could be said for Grace herself. Hopefully, she and Cole would marry one day. The dynamics would change whether they lived at the house, the farm, or both. These were positive things, yet they still carried an air of sadness. As someone who had, until recently, lived a very lonely life, she enjoyed being surrounded by people every day. Losing that will be hard.

A knock on the door interrupted Grace's reverie. She gave Rebekah a confused look. "Who could that be?"

"Molly and Grant?" she asked.

"I don't think so. They haven't knocked since the first time they showed up here."

"Only one way to find out," Rebekah shrugged.

Rebekah followed Grace to the front door, where they found Evie on the other side.

"What's up?" Grace asked cautiously. The few times Evie had shown up during the middle of the day, something had been wrong.

"Can I come in?" she asked, a look of exasperation on her face.

"Of course," Grace stepped back to make room for her to enter the foyer, then followed Evie and Rebekah back to the dining room. "Is everything okay?" she asked once they sat down.

"No, everything is not okay," Evie sighed. "My sister is driving me crazy, and if you guys don't do something to help me, I may have to leave town!"

Grace and Rebekah exchanged looks. "While we are always happy to help a friend in need, I'm not sure what we can do to help with Shelley," Grace replied carefully.

"I didn't know you were even on speaking terms," replied Rebekah. "Did something change in that regard?"

"Not on my part, but Shelley never has cared about other people's feelings. Now that our parents have kicked her out, she's been trying to convince Jake and me to take her in. Worse than that, we've caught her out on our property doing the craziest stunts. Just yesterday, she was trying to zip-line into the lake from a power line that doesn't even go into the water!"

"A couple of days ago, Cole and I caught her trying to ride one of his bulls. She was almost trampled!" Grace shook her head. "This social media stuff has caused her to lose what little sense she had."

Rebekah got up and went into the kitchen to grab a plate of cookies and a pitcher of lemonade. When she returned, she set them in the middle of the table so everyone could help themselves. "I agree that something needs to be done," Rebekah began as she selected a cookie. "But what do you think we can do? There is no way Shelley would listen to one of us."

Evie silently picked at a cookie as she thought of a response. "She needs a job. Something that would occupy her time and give her something to do that isn't dangerous."

"Oh no," Grace held up her hands. "There is no way I'm hiring Shelley to work for me."

"Yeah, I'm sorry, Evie, but I'm going to have to pass as well," Rebekah said quickly. "After what she tried to do to you, I can't have her anywhere near my wedding clients."

"Come on, guys, there has to be something," Evie said in frustration.

"Where is her baby?" asked Grace. She was genuinely concerned for the safety of that poor, innocent child.

"Living with the father, and, get this, Greg's ex, Jessica."

Grace and Rebekah raised their brows in surprise. "Jesse got full custody?" Grace asked.

Evie nodded. "He didn't even have to fight for it. Once Shelley had that video go viral, she just handed him the baby. She told him she didn't have time to be a mom. That was when my parents kicked her out for good."

"That's not the story she tells, though I'm not surprised," said Grace. "So Greg gave up his baby, too?"

"As far as I know, Greg left town after he got arrested for the stunts he pulled at the hotel last Summer. It sounds bad that they abandoned their kids, but let's face it: those kids are better off without them. I have never known two people less fit to be parents than those two," said Evie. She took a deep breath and let it out slowly. "Jake and I are still in their lives if you're wondering. We have a good relationship with Jesse and Jessica, and they have allowed us to see the babies whenever we want."

Evie's face lit up as she talked about the kids. At least there was one bright spot in that mess.

"That's awesome, Evie," Grace said enthusiastically. "But about Shelley, I just don't see how we can help. Unless..." she trailed off as a thought occurred to her.

"Unless what?" Evie sat up straight and stared at Grace hopefully.

There was no doubt in her mind she would regret this. But, if she were going to do a haunted hotel, she would need help, and now that Molly was on maternity leave, that left few options. Her mind made up, she filled them in on her plan. "I need someone to play a ghost in the hotel," Grace began. "Since Shelley already has some experience with that, she might be a good choice to fill the role."

"Oh," Evie sat back, a deflated look on her face. "She'll never go for that."

"Don't be so sure," said Rebekah. "If we told her it's a starring role and that she could post videos on her social media accounts, she might do it. It might also give us the added benefit of free advertisement since she does have a decent following."

"You really think so," Evie asked. It was obvious she was not convinced, but a spark of hope was starting to peek through her uncertainty. Or maybe it was desperation.

"Why don't we talk to her and see what she says?" Grace suggested. "Who knows, she might surprise us all."

Evie nodded. "Okay, I'll call her and arrange a meeting." She gave a small smile and then stood up. "Thanks, guys. I really appreciate it."

"No problem," said Grace.

Grace waited to hear the front door open and close, then turned to Rebekah. "I'm going to regret this, aren't I?"

"Oh yeah," she replied. "Big time!"

***

For the first time in days, Grace had the house to herself. Rebekah was out at the winery working on the wedding, Molly, Grant, and Eliza were resting peacefully next door, and Granny and Gladys were sewing happily in Granny's room. Which meant it was time for more decorations!

After checking on everyone one last time, Grace grabbed her paint supplies and headed outside. It was time to tackle her spooky band project. She still wasn't sure how she would create a band out of hay, but the longer she stared at the bales, the closer she got to an idea.

Finally, inspiration struck! Scarecrows! She could take old clothes, stuff them with hay, and make scarecrows. Then, she could make smaller bales from the bigger ones to create a drum set. The guitars could be fashioned out of cardboard boxes, and the microphones out of foil and large, spray-painted sticks. Now, she just had to hope it didn't rain.

She gathered all the supplies she would need and set to work. She was so engrossed in her project she didn't hear Cole pull up in his truck despite its loud diesel engine. When a pair of strong arms wrapped around her from behind, she was so startled she dropped her scarecrow, screamed, and jumped back into said arms.

"It's just me," Cole said as he steadied her back on her feet. He chuckled as he kissed her ear. "I didn't mean to scare you, darlin'. I thought you would have heard me pull up," he drawled.

Grace took a deep breath and relaxed into his embrace. "Sorry, I wasn't paying attention. I'm pretty sure a freight train could have passed by me, and I wouldn't have noticed," she laughed.

"I see," he said as he nuzzled the side of her neck. "What are you working on?"

He was making it difficult to think; as usual, she was sure he knew it. "I'm making a scarecrow band out of the hay you brought me," she said, her arms tightening around his. "I thought you had errands to run today?"

"I did, but now I'm done, so I thought I'd come hang out with you," he replied.

"Want to help me?" she asked.

"If I say yes, does that mean I have to let go?" he asked huskily.

She laughed; if he didn't let go soon, her neighbors would complain. She turned in his arms and kissed him properly. "How about you help me, and then we can go to your place, and I'll help you."

"Deal," he replied, kissing the tip of her nose. "Show me what you want me to do, and then consider it done. Although, just so you know, this is straw, not hay."

"Does it matter?" she asked.

"Depends on who you're talking to," he shrugged.

It took them two hours to finish the band, but when they finished, they stood back arm in arm as they admired the results. Of course, a scarecrow band was more silly than scary, but that was precisely how Grace wanted it to be. The house was coming together, and she just knew her guests would love it.

"Ready to head to your place?" she asked Cole.

"Sure am," he pulled her close to him. "What time do you need to be back?"

"Not until tomorrow morning," she answered.

Cole raised his brow. "Really?"

"Yep, it's Rebekah's night to cook."

"In that case," he led her to his truck, opened the passenger door, and helped her climb in.

Grace automatically slid to the middle of the seat as he climbed into the driver's side. The closer they got to the ranch, the more she felt she was going home. Was it the ranch making her feel that way? Or was it Cole? She had a feeling it was a bit of both.

-Days till Halloween-

Fifteen

Grace was in the kitchen getting breakfast ready when Rebekah walked in.

"Hey, you're back," said Rebekah.

"Did you miss me?" asked Grace.

"Of course," smiled Rebekah. "How was your night with Cole?"

How did one answer a question like that? "It was fun," Grace said, hoping that would be the end of it.

"Great! We have a lot of work to do, starting with a meeting at the mayor's office in thirty minutes."

Grace checked her watch, then looked around at the food she was only half-done cooking. "Guess I better hurry up," she muttered.

Rebekah walked beside her and grabbed an apron off one of the hooks near the pantry. "Let me help so we can get it done faster."

"What's the meeting about?" Grace asked, curious as to why she was being dragged into a meeting with the mayor.

Last she checked, she hadn't been planning anything to warrant that.

"The Halloween Fair, duh," Rebekah replied, bumping Grace with her hip.

Had that been her idea? For some reason, she couldn't remember. She would have to find time to take a real vacation someday. "I thought that was just a passing idea," said Grace. "There's only about two weeks left until Halloween. Do we even have time to arrange something as big as a fair?"

"Usually, the answer would be no, but I made some calls and found a company with a last-minute cancellation. They were more than happy to give the slot to us since Halloween is usually a big money-maker for them."

Grace eyed her friend out of the corner of her eye. "Did you forget to tell them how big our town is? Or rather, how small?" Grace asked suspiciously.

"I didn't lie if that's what you're asking," Rebekah replied. "People are always looking for places to go on holidays; I have zero doubts we'll be able to draw a huge crowd with the right marketing."

Maybe she was right, maybe she wasn't; at this point, it didn't matter. "Is the meeting with the town council or just Mayor Allen?" Grace asked curiously.

"The whole council. We need them to vote so we can finalize the plans. That shouldn't be a problem, should it?"

"I doubt it. They're usually more than willing to go along with whatever we propose if it brings in money. Speaking of which, we need to discuss the upcoming wedding, specifically the part about feeding the guests at the hotel."

Rebekah looked at her in surprise. "Isn't that between you, Molly, and Grant?"

"Yes, but now that they're busy with the baby, I'm on my own." Grace looked at Rebekah expectantly.

"Okay, what exactly is the problem? Didn't the kitchen pass inspection?"

"Again, yes, but—"

"But what?" Rebekah exclaimed, interrupting her. "Grace, I need you to spit it out because I'm not following you right now."

Grace rolled her eyes in frustration. "But—," she began again. "I'm only one person. I don't have time to run the hotel, run the B&B, cook at the hotel, cook at the B&B, run the haunted hotel attraction, and run the Halloween Fair."

"I'm supposed to be in charge of the fair," she reminded Grace.

"Fine, whatever, that still leaves everything else."

Rebekah opened her mouth to respond, then closed it again. She appeared to be deep in thought. "Is there anyone we can ask to help?" she finally said.

Grace shook her head. "Molly and Grant are out, Gladys and Granny aren't healthy enough, Emilio already has his plate full covering for Grant, and everyone else has full-time jobs. Including you."

"What about Cole and Riley?"

Grace shook her head a second time. "Even though things have slowed down, they're still pretty busy. I'm sure they'll help when and where they can, but they can't be counted on for the kind of help I will need."

Rebekah sighed. "I'd offer to help, and of course I will when I can, but I'm concerned I'm going to be too busy

with the fair and the wedding to be much good either."
She grabbed plates out of the cabinet and set them on the
counter. "We're going to have to hire someone."

The timer on the oven dinged, causing Grace to imagine
a light bulb going off like in the movies. She grabbed an
oven mitt and carefully pulled the egg casserole out. "I've
thought about that," she explained to Rebekah. "But how
does that work when your business is seasonal? The employee would have to be someone local who doesn't need
steady employment. Do those even exist?"

"If you're willing to do the cooking, I'm sure you can
find someone willing to do the cleaning."

They finished setting out the rest of the food just in time
for the breakfast group to arrive. Even without Molly and
Grant, it was still a full house with Emilio, Cole, and Riley
joining them. As she handed out plates, Grace thought
about what Rebekah said. She still wasn't convinced but
figured it was best to try before allowing the problem to
stress her out further. There were plenty of other things to
stress over!

***

Grace and Rebekah were the last to arrive, the rest of
the group already seated and talking quietly among themselves. They sheepishly took their seats, avoiding Mayor
Allen's gaze as he impatiently tapped his watch.

"Ladies," he said to Grace and Rebekah. "Since you two
are the reason for this meeting, please get started."

Rebekah cleared her throat. "Sorry," she said to Mayor
Allen. She then turned to address the rest of the people in

the room. "Grace and I would like to bring the annual fair back to Winterwood."

Bea, Junior, Addie, and Mr. Wilkins stared in their direction.

"It's a little late for this year. Is this something you're trying to plan for next year?" asked Bea. She appeared confused as if this was not what she had expected.

"Actually, we would like to do it October twenty-ninth through the thirty-first," Rebekah explained.

"But we've always done the fair in August," said Addie. "Besides, this is way too short notice. It will be impossible to get a carnival group here in the next two weeks."

Rebekah cleared her throat again and looked to Grace for help. "Rebekah already found someone willing to come," Grace explained. She smiled at them as she tried to drum up some excitement. "There was a last-minute cancellation, so the spot is ours if we move quickly."

"I don't know," Bea said hesitantly.

"What's the problem?" asked Mr. Wilkins. "We did far more in less time last Christmas. This should be a piece of cake."

"You think so?" asked Bea. "Because I'm already pretty swamped with orders from school parties."

Bea's attitude was a big surprise to Grace. The older woman was usually the first one on board regarding these things. Something must be wrong. "You don't have to participate if you don't want to," Grace said gently. "There will be plenty of food trucks and street vendors to fill the gap."

"I suppose you're right," Bea conceded. "But Grace, aren't you and Rebekah already over-extended right now?

We've heard about the big Halloween-themed wedding you're doing."

"We were hoping this would help with that," said Rebekah. "The fair would give the guests something to do, which would lighten Grace's load, plus it would draw a large crowd, which would be good for the haunted hotel attraction she's putting on."

Addie shook her head. "How you girls find the time to do all this is beyond me," she exclaimed.

"About that," Grace began. "I could use some help at the hotel and B&B. Do any of you know someone who would be interested in some part-time seasonal work?"

"I do," said Mr. Wilkins. He glanced at Mayor Allen, who did not appear pleased by the change in topic. "We can talk after the meeting," he said quickly.

"So," said Mayor Allen. "Are there any more questions, or are we ready to vote?"

They all looked around the room, and when no one spoke up, Mayor Allen continued. "Good, looks like we're ready to vote. All in favor say, "Aye."

"Aye," came a chorus of replies.

"Any nays?" he asked as he looked around. "No? Good." He turned to face Rebekah and Grace. "Will we need a committee for this, or can you two handle it?"

"A committee of volunteers would be helpful," said Grace. "We'll need to decorate the town for Halloween, put together a panel of judges for the costume contest, and come up with a couple more events for the town."

"You can use my restaurant again," Addie volunteered. "That's worked out pretty well in the past, so I don't see a reason to change it."

"Thank you," said Grace.

"I'll send out a message on the town's social media page," said Rebekah. "I'm sure we can handle things from here, Mayor Allen."

"Good," he nodded at her approvingly. "Let me know if there is anything you need from me. Have a good day, everyone."

He was out the door before they could say goodbye. As the mayor, pastor, and town realtor, he was always on the go, too busy to stay in one place for long. Grace did not envy him, though she probably had more in common with him than she would admit.

Mr. Wilkins walked over and sat down next to them. "So, about that part-time job," he began. "How many hours are we talking?"

"I only need someone for about two weeks," Grace said, wincing as she heard the words come out of her mouth. "Will that be a problem?"

"What kind of work will it be?"

"I need someone to help me prepare the hotel and B&B for the guests and do daily cleaning once they check in. I could also use some help in the kitchen, washing dishes, setting and clearing tables, that kind of thing. Is that okay?"

"If that's what you need, I don't see why not," he replied. "My granddaughter is staying with me right now. She's been helping out around the store, but she gets bored, and I feel she would like this a lot more. She needs busy work, you know?"

Yes, she did know. Busy work got her through many stressful times over the last year. It caused a lot of stress as well. "Do you think she could meet me at the hotel tomorrow morning? I could show her around and see what she thinks?" asked Grace.

"Sure, I'll send her over after the meeting. Her name's Jillian, though her Grandma and I have always called her Jilly."

He stood up and moved toward the door, Grace and Rebekah following. She had wanted to talk to Bea, but she appeared to have left while they were talking to Mr. Wilkins. She would have to make the trip to her farm if she couldn't catch her at the bakery later that afternoon.

"I need to head to the winery," said Rebekah. "Want me to drop you off at home before I go?"

"Nah, I can walk. It's such a beautiful day; I better take advantage of it while I can."

Rebekah nodded. "Sounds good; I'll see you tonight then."

They parted and went their separate ways, Rebekah to her car and Grace toward the home. As she walked, she tried to picture Jilly in her mind. For some reason, she kept picturing a young teenager and hoped that wasn't the case. Not that she had anything against teenagers; it's just it would be nice to have someone with a bit more work experience than that. Guests could be demanding, and one had to keep a cool head.

When she got home, she went next door to check on Molly and the baby. According to Grant, who appeared to be working from home, they were sleeping, so she left quietly, careful not to disturb them. She was dying to finally hold little Eliza, but that would have to wait. Oh well, plenty of time for that later.

-Days till Halloween-

Fourteen

Addie's Diner was practically bursting at the seams when Grace and Rebekah arrived for the morning meeting. Stunned, Grace turned to Rebekah. "Are all these people here to help with the fair?"

Rebekah looked just as surprised as Grace. "You would know more than I would. Has there been this kind of turn-out in the past?"

Grace thought back to the first time they'd done this last Christmas. "Yeah, but not quite like this. Guess we better hurry up and get in there; Mayor Allen is likely chomping at the bit to get started."

They rushed inside, discovering the true cause of the turn-out: Addie's breakfast special. For two dollars, you could get a cup of coffee and a breakfast burrito, both known to be the best in town. Disappointed, Grace hurried over to the counter where Bea and Addie were busy serving the pre-made items.

"It must feel pretty good to know your burritos command this kind of attention," Grace teased Addie.

Addie shrugged. "As long as they help command the kind of help we need, I'm all for it. If all these people do is eat and leave, I will be very disappointed."

"I hear you," said Grace, choosing a sausage and egg burrito. "Although, if we can get even half as many volunteers as last Christmas, I think we'll be okay."

"I hope you're right," said Bea. "The carnival folks will set up the rides, but the business owners are responsible for creating the atmosphere. There's almost as much decorating to do as last time."

"We'll get it done," Grace reassured her. Bea's concern had Grace concerned. Usually, Bea was a very positive person who was always first in line to volunteer. In fact, she had always been Grace's biggest supporter. Something must be really wrong.

The sound of a spoon tapping on glass interrupted their conversation, all eyes turning to the front of the room where Mayor Allen stood. Once the room had gone silent, he cleared his throat and addressed them. "I must say, I'm thrilled to see so many of you here willing to help out your community. In the interest of time, I'm going to turn this over to Grace and Rebekah so they can share the details with you."

The first time Mayor Allen had put her on the spot, Grace had been completely caught off guard. This time, she was ready—to hand it over to Rebekah so she could be the one in the spotlight for a change. After all, she was much better suited for it anyway.

As Grace nudged her forward, Rebekah gave her a dirty look but dutifully stepped up to address the crowd. "Good morning, everyone," she said cheerfully. "As Mayor Allen said, we appreciate you coming out this morning. If you haven't heard, we are bringing the annual fair back to town for Halloween, and we need volunteers to help in several areas."

"Are you bringing back the parade as well?" asked Principal Adams.

Grace looked around the room, spotting him back by the door. Principal Adams had been instrumental in helping out with the various holiday activities they'd planned throughout the last year. More than once, he'd allowed some of the older high schoolers to help out for extra credit and some of the school clubs to partner with those in the community to support and assist with some of their community programs. If he was involved, their chance of success just went up exponentially.

Rebekah looked to Grace for help. "Um, I didn't know you usually did a parade. Grace?"

Grace had forgotten about the parade. She had been in middle school the last time the town had put on the fair. But at that time, the fair was in August, and the parade was usually held on the last day, which was typically Saturday. "Since Halloween is on a Tuesday this year, the fair will run Sunday through Tuesday," Grace explained. "Which I know is a little unorthodox," she said, holding out her hands to quiet the protesting crowd's objections.

Mayor Allen clinked the spoon and glass together again. "Quiet," he yelled above the noise. When everyone finally settled down, he gave the floor back to Grace.

"As I was saying," she began. "I realize this is a little unorthodox, but we don't control the calendar. That being said, it's up to you all if we do the parade."

"We should put it to a vote," said the mayor. "All in favor, say aye."

A thunderous "aye" erupted from the crowd. Who could have guessed so many people liked parades? Not Grace. She had expected a thunderous nay. Had actually been hoping for nay. A parade was one more thing they had to worry about on a never-ending list of things to worry about.

"Looks like the ayes have it," said Mayor Allen. "Principal Adams," he said, addressing the man. "Can we count on the school's involvement in bringing this parade to life?"

"Of course," he replied. "You know the students will jump on any opportunity to get out of classwork!"

The group laughed, many of them nodding earnestly, likely thinking back to their school days.

"Wonderful," said Mayor Allen. He turned to face Grace and Rebekah. "Anything else, ladies?" he asked.

"Sign-up sheets are by the door, and we would appreciate it if you would sign up for any and all committees you wish to join before leaving," said Rebekah.

"You heard the woman," he told the crowd. "Thank you again; we look forward to working together to make this the best Halloween ever!"

Mayor Allen made a beeline for the door, pausing briefly to chat with Principal Adams before following him outside. Grace watched, envious of his ability to flee crowded rooms without being stopped by at least a dozen people on the way out. Someday, she would learn his tricks. Today, she would accept her fate and do her best to patiently greet her fellow friends and neighbors.

***

It had taken almost an hour to get out of Addie's, but she had finally managed to do it, just in time to meet Jillian at the hotel. As she approached the hotel, she saw a woman with long dark hair pulled back in a braid waiting by the door. The woman appeared to be in her thirties, though one can never tell for sure. It made sense, though, now that she thought about it. A teenager would be in school, not applying for cleaning jobs.

"I'm so sorry to keep you waiting," Grace said as he held out her hand to the woman.

"No problem," the woman smiled, shaking her hand. "I was a little early."

"I'm Grace," she said, introducing herself. "I'm assuming you're Jillian?"

"Yes, though most people call me Jilly."

"It's nice to meet you, Jilly," Grace said warmly. She could already tell she was going to like the woman. Now, she just had to hope the woman liked her in return. She pulled her keys out of her purse and unlocked the front door, holding it open so Jilly could enter first.

"Wow, this place is incredible!" Jilly said with a whistle. "I feel like I've stepped into a time machine and ended up back in the eighteen hundreds."

Grace looked around the lobby and tried to see it with fresh eyes. The red granite floors were immaculate, the white walls were freshly painted, but those things were standard and expected at all hotels. What wasn't standard was the floor-to-ceiling columns, the marble fireplace, or the ornate trim molding everywhere. A sense of pride came over her as she admired all the work she had done to bring this place back to life.

"Thank you," Grace said with a smile. "Our goal was restoration wherever possible. If you check the history book at the library, you'll see we achieved that goal."

Jilly continued wandering from room to room, Grace trailing behind as she pointed out what she would need Jilly to do each day. They finished the tour back in the lobby, Grace offering her hopefully new employee a chair in front of the fireplace. "What brings you to Winter-wood?" she asked.

Pain flashed across Jilly's face. She took a moment to compose herself before answering. "My husband recent-ly passed away quite unexpectedly. He was only thir-ty-six," she explained, tears filling her eyes. "I was strug-gling to cope with his loss and our two young kids by myself, so when my grandpa offered to let us stay with him, I gladly accepted."

"I am so sorry for your loss," Grace said gently. Her thoughts flashed to Cole, and she struggled to hold back her own tears at the thought of losing him. "Are you sure you want to do this?" she asked. "If you're not ready—"

"Please," Jilly interrupted. "I love my grandpa, but his store isn't close to busy enough to warrant two employ-ees. I need something that will keep me busy. That will keep my mind off...things I'd rather not think about."

"Okay," Grace nodded, her heart aching for the woman. "We need help over at the B&B as well. Plus, there's the haunted hotel on the third floor. You'll be busier than a bee in springtime between the three of them!"

Jilly laughed. "That sounds perfect, thank you, Grace."

Grace had never hired anyone before or had a real job, so she was still trying to figure out what to do. Molly would know, but she didn't want to bother her in case she was sleeping. So, what should she do? Call Emilio. He would have the answers.

"Excuse me for just one minute," Grace said. She stood up and walked over to the check-in desk, pulling out her phone as she went. Seconds later, Emilio was on the phone. "Hey," she said. "I'm interviewing a new employee at the hotel and want to hire her. Can you help me?"

"Sure," he replied. "What do you need?"

"I was kind of hoping you could tell me. Do I need her to fill out paperwork or something?" That's what they did in the movies, isn't it?

"Hang tight, and I'll be there in about fifteen minutes."

Grace looked at her phone. He had hung up without saying goodbye. What is it with people these days? She shook her head; she would never understand the ever-changing trends if that's what this was. She walked back over to Jilly and resumed her seat.

"Do you have a few minutes?" she asked her. "Emilio is on his way with some paperwork for you to fill out."

"Sure," she replied. "I doubt I'm missing out on much at the store."

They chatted about the upcoming fair and the guests Grace expected to be checking in. She did her best to avoid discussing the wedding, a topic she assumed would be painful for her new employee. It would be difficult to avoid it altogether, but she would do her best.

Thankfully, Emilio was faster than he had predicted, showing up just in time to help them avoid an awkward lull in the conversation. "Here is everything you need," he

said to Grace, handing her a manila folder full of paperwork."

Grace took it and handed it to Jilly, who she hoped
had more experience with these things than Grace did.
"Thanks, Emilio, you're the best," she smiled.

"No problem; let me know if you need anything else."

"Should I return these to you when we're done here?"
Grace asked.

"Yes, please, I'll be handling all the payroll stuff until
Grant returns from parental leave."

"Do you know when that will be?" Grace asked, curious
how long he planned to stay away from his new business.

"Supposedly, he's going to be gone until the first of De-
cember, but you know Grant," he shrugged.

"Yeah," she replied. She didn't have to say anymore. They
both knew Grant was a workaholic; no need to say it out
loud.

When Jilly finished her paperwork, Grace walked her to
the door. "Can you start tomorrow? There is a lot to do
and very little time to do it."

"Sure, should I meet you here first thing in the morning?"

"That would be great. Thanks Jilly."

"You're welcome, Grace. See you tomorrow."

"See you tomorrow."

-Days till Halloween-

Thirteen

After Grace got Jilly set up at the hotel, she went home to work on the B&B. She still had some decorating to finish in addition to the menu she needed to plan. When she got there, she went to check on Granny and Gladys.

The first thing she noticed when she entered Granny's room was Piper happily rolling around with a ball of yarn at their feet. The second thing she noticed was the big smile on Granny's face as she sat at the sewing machine. It had been a long time since she had seen Granny this happy.

"What are you working on?" Grace asked, her curiosity piqued.

"It's a surprise," Granny said mysteriously.

"Oh, come on, Granny. You know you can tell me anything," Grace persisted.

"Anything but what this surprise is," Granny said mischievously.

"Seriously, Grace. Let us old gals have a little fun!" Gladys teased her. She, too, was sitting at a sewing machine, facing Granny as they worked.

"Okay," Grace sighed dramatically "Have it your way." She sat down on the bed and watched them for a minute, hoping if she sat there long enough, she would figure out what they were doing. When that didn't happen, she gave up. "When did you learn to sew?" she asked Granny.

"Oh, let's see," Granny said, taking her hands off the fabric and placing them in her lap. "I believe I was around eight years old when Mama first taught me how to darn socks," she said, her eyes glazing over a little as she searched her memories. "Once I mastered that, she taught me how to make simple dresses. By the time I was your age, I had a job working as a seamstress in a curtain store."

Grace searched her memories for talk of Granny's job as a seamstress. She had always assumed her grandmother had been a stay-at-home wife and mother, living off her husband's social security benefits after he died. Now that she thought about it, that didn't make sense. "How come you never told me this before?" she asked.

"I guess it never came up," Granny shrugged.

"You gave up your job because of me, didn't you?" asked Grace. She felt ashamed that she had been the cause of her beloved grandmother giving up a job she so obviously loved.

Granny reached over and took her hand. "None of that," she said firmly. "You were not the cause of the end of my career. By the time you came around, decades had passed since they closed the curtain stores. We lost our jobs to factories; we could not compete with cheap labor. From time to time, I could still take on the odd job here and there, usually wedding dress alterations, but those were few and far between in a town this size."

"Why didn't you make clothes for me?" asked Grace.

"I would have loved that," Granny sighed. "But fabric is expensive, and you out-grew your clothes too fast to make anything other than thrift store bargains affordable. I have hoped—" Granny abruptly stopped talking and resumed her sewing.

"Had hoped what?" Grace asked.

"Yeah, Josie, what were you going to say?" asked Gladys.

"It's nothing," she smiled, gazing at the machine before her.

"Granny," Grace groaned. "You can't leave us hanging like that!"

Granny lifted her head to look at Grace. "I just— I don't want to put any pressure on you."

"I can't imagine you ever doing that," Grace said gently.

"In that case, I was hoping that I could make your wedding dress." Granny sucked in a breath while she waited for Grace's reaction.

Sensing how important this was to her, Grace wrapped her arms around Granny's shoulders. "I would love that," she said as she hugged her tightly. Nothing could be more special than walking down the aisle in a dress her grandmother had made her. Especially if Cole was waiting for her at the end of that aisle.

All her childhood memories of hating her Halloween costumes came rushing back, flooding her cheeks with embarrassment at how petty she had been. Those costumes had been a highlight of Granny's life. An opportunity to share her joy and passion and Grace had treated them with disdain. Oh, how she wished she could go back and do things over. Unfortunately, she would have to make do with showing her appreciation moving forward.

She carefully scooped up Piper, ball of yarn and all, and snuggled her close for a moment. Her fluffy black and white fur tickled Grace's nose, causing her to sneeze, which startled Piper and made her jump out of Grace's arms and run under the bed. Ruby, lying in her bed by the window, opened her eyes, yawned and stretched, then went back to sleep, not a care in her little dog world.

"Well," Grace said to the room. "It looks like things are under control here, so I'll leave you to it."

"Sounds good, dear," Granny said absentmindedly.

Grace chuckled, delighted to see the changes in her grandmother. From this day forward, every holiday would require a costume. Anything to keep the joy on her grandmother's face.

***

Evie finally convinced Shelley to meet with Grace and Rebekah regarding the haunted hotel. Why Shelley fought so hard against it was anyone's guess. When it came to Shelley, things rarely made sense.

Grace hadn't had time to start on the decorations for the third floor, but the lack of sunlight, the thick layer of dust on every available surface, and the dingy décor from the sixties did a pretty good job of creating a haunted atmosphere. It was not hard to imagine a ghost wandering the dark halls or staring morosely out of one of the old, grimy windows.

When Grace arrived at the hotel, Jilly was still working her way through the downstairs rooms, so she invited her to the third floor to meet with Shelley. After all, if Shelley agreed, Jilly would have to put up with her, too.

Once on the third floor, they discovered Rebekah and Shelley waiting, the latter rather impatiently.

"It's about time," she said to Grace. "I still have videos to film for the day, so this better not take long." Shelley was, once again, wearing a wedding dress.

"Out of curiosity," Grace said, ignoring her snarky comments. "Is that the same dress, or do you have a collection?"

Shelley rolled her eyes. "As if. I would never wear the same dress twice."

"Where are you getting all those dresses?" asked Jilly, her eyes wide. "When I married, I spent nearly five thousand on mine."

"Thrift stores," Shelley shrugged. "Now, if you don't mind, what do you want?"

It took all of her strength not to kick Shelley out of the hotel and ban her for life. Grace would do this without thinking twice if she were doing it for anyone other than Evie. As it was, she still felt she owed her after all the problems they had with her wedding last July. After this, however, they would be even. More than even.

"Shelley," Rebekah began with a strained smile. "Since you are such a great actress, we would like to offer you the starring role as the ghost of Ms. Hathaway for the haunted hotel event we're putting on."

"Who's Ms. Hathaway?" she asked, her eyes narrowed as she gazed at Rebekah suspiciously.

"Ms. Hathaway is a young woman believed to haunt this hotel," Grace explained. "Back in the eighteen-sixties, she was supposed to meet her beau here, the son of a wealthy cattle rancher. His father disapproved of their relationship, so they planned to take the train out west and start a new life together, far away from his father's influence. Legend has it that right before they were to board the train, his father showed up with another young woman claiming to carry the beau's baby. Not wanting to abandon his child, the beau left Ms. Hathaway and returned with his father and the other young woman. Her heart broken, she threw herself on the tracks and ended her life."

"That's horrible," said Jilly.

"Is that too much?" Grace asked her. "We could always change it to Ms. Hathaway taking a bottle of sleeping pills in one of the rooms if you think that would be less gruesome?"

"It would make more sense for her to haunt this floor," said Rebekah.

Grace thought about that. "Good point." She turned to Shelley. "What do you think? Do you want to be Ms. Hathaway?"

"What's in it for me?" Shelley asked.

"Well, for starters, you can post tons of 'backstage' content on your social media accounts that shows you getting ready for opening night. Then, you can film the events and post that as well," explained Grace.

Grace watched the wheels turn in Shelley's head. She was hard to predict; Grace had no clue which way she would go; she could only hope for the best.

"Fine, but I also want five percent of the ticket sales," Shelley said.

"Deal," Grace said quickly. Do you know a few more people interested in acting out the infamous showdown with you?

"I could probably come up with a few volunteers," she mused. "When do we open?"

"The Friday before Halloween," said Grace. "So you have eight days to prepare."

"I'm going to need a new dress," Shelley announced. "Something, period. A ghost from the eighteen-sixties would not haunt the hotel in a modern-day wedding dress."

Grace and Rebekah exchanged glances. Unfortunately, Shelley was right. The others would need costumes as well. "Get your group of actors together, and I'll see what I can do," said Grace. "Just make sure you do it quickly. If I have to order costumes online, and I probably will, we'll need time for them to arrive."

"Fine," Shelley said, rolling her eyes. "I'll let you know tomorrow morning. Just so you know, I want a real costume, not some box store cheapo. My adoring fans have come to expect a certain level of quality from me, and I will not compromise that for you," she sniffed.

It was Grace's turn to roll her eyes. "Fine, fine," she said, waving her hand dismissively. "We'll see you tomorrow."

Once Shelley was safely out of earshot, Grace turned to Rebekah and Jilly. "That
woman," she said, shaking her head.

"Are you sure Evie wasn't adopted?" asked Rebekah. "It's tough to believe they come from the same family."

"You're not kidding," said Grace. "You think you'll be able to handle her?" Grace asked Jilly.

"I'm a mom of two toddlers," Jilly replied. "I can handle a third."

Grace snorted. "I knew I was going to like you," she told Jilly.

The three of them spent the next hour reviewing the third-floor layout and planning the decorations they would put up. Since they planned to go with more of a haunted western theme, they would avoid the usual spiderwebs, black cats, and scary monsters typical of haunted houses and lean more into period-appropriate props and attire.

Grace wanted the style to be closer to that of "Rebecca" or "The House of Usher" rather than "Nightmare on Elm Street." They would be different, but sometimes, going against expectations is good. Sometimes, real life is scarier than fiction.

-Days till Halloween-

Twelve

"How are things going with Jilly?" Gladys asked over breakfast.

Startled, Grace dropped her fork and turned to Gladys. She had been lost in a daydream, or maybe a waking nightmare was more accurate. All she knew was that Shelley was driving her crazy. For no reason other than to annoy Grace, Shelley had called her at two o'clock in the morning to inform her that she and a group of friends would meet her at the hotel around eleven. Eleven o'clock! She couldn't have waited until eight or nine to call? Of course not; that would be asking too much.

"Sorry, Gladys, what did you say?" asked Grace. It had taken over an hour to fall back asleep, and she was tired. Tired and horrified at the thought that Shelley might keep this up for the next two weeks for no other reason than she could.

"I asked how things were going with Jilly," Gladys repeated. "Are you okay, dear?"

"I'm fine, thanks. It's only been one day, but things with Jilly are great. She's a hard worker and has already contributed a lot of great ideas. I'm going to miss her when this is all over."

Gladys nodded. "That business with her husband was so sad. He was only thirty-six years old and died of a heart attack. It's tragic," she sighed.

"A heart attack? Really?" asked Grace. She had assumed he'd been in a car accident like her parents.

"He worked a high-stress, demanding job. Drank way too much caffeine, ate way too much processed food, no exercise, you know the drill," Gladys explained.

"That's so sad," said Grace. Regardless of how or why, someone's beloved husband, father, son, etc., died, and she felt terrible for their loss.

"Something for you and your young man to consider," said Gladys. "Life is too short for you two to work yourselves to death. If you're not careful, you could end up like Jilly."

Grace's eyes went wide at the mere thought of losing Cole. She wanted to believe they were different, but Jilly and her husband probably thought the same thing, and well, look at them. No, Gladys was right; things needed to change before something life-changing occurred.

"What time are you meeting Shelley?" Rebekah asked in an attempt to steer the conversation to safer topics.

She gave her a grateful smile before answering. "Eleven o'clock. Shelley claims she has friends lined up to play the other parts."

"What are the chances these so-called friends will show up?" Rebekah asked doubtfully.

"Who knows," Grace sighed. "We should probably devise a plan B just in case."

"I bet Riley and Katie would be willing to play the part of the beau and his pregnant mistress," Rebekah speculated. "That just leaves the part of the disapproving father."

Grace looked around the table. "Anyone got any suggestions?"

"What about Mayor Allen?" asked Granny. "He's a little too young to be Riley's father, but with the right costume and lighting, I doubt anyone would notice."

"He's swamped," said Grace. "Do you really think he would agree?"

"Only one way to find out," said Granny.

"Any other ideas?" Grace asked. "Just in case?"

"I suppose I could ask Thorne," Rebekah replied hesitantly. "He's been swamped, though, so I feel like giving up five nights is a lot to ask right now."

"That's okay," said Grace. "I'll talk to the mayor, and if he isn't available, maybe he'll know someone who is."

Grace stood up and began to clear the table. "I need to get going if I'm going to catch him in his office," she said to no one in particular. She carried the plates to the sink and quickly loaded them into the dishwasher. "I'll see you guys later," she said on her way out the door.

"Wait," Rebekah called out. She rushed into the foyer as Grace opened the door. "I'll drop you off on the way to the winery," she told Grace.

"It's okay, I can walk," said Grace.

"I need to talk to you," Rebekah explained.

They walked silently to the car, each getting in on their respective sides. "So, what's up?" Grace asked once they were on the road.

"Are you okay?" Rebekah asked. "I saw how upset you got when Gladys commented about you and Cole."

Grace sighed and looked out the window. She had passed these same houses hundreds if not thousands of times, yet she never got tired of looking at them. They were familiar, bringing a sense of peace and home.

"She didn't say anything I haven't been thinking for a while now. It just hurt to hear it said out loud. Cole and I need to make some changes if we have any kind of future together; I just don't know what changes we can realistically make. Work needs to be done, animals need to be fed, and Granny and Gladys need to be cared for. Those things can't change, so what do we do?"

Rebekah parked in front of city hall and turned to face Grace. "At this point, you have two choices: change careers or hire more help. I know that might be hard, but I'm sure there's a way as long as there's a will."

Grace smiled at the somewhat backward but ultimately accurate saying. "You're right," she admitted. "Cole and I need to sit down and have a real discussion about this."

"With Emilio," said Rebekah.

"Emilio? Why?" Grace furrowed her brow at the unexpected suggestion.

"Because silly, he's an expert at these kinds of things. Why pass up an opportunity to get valuable and, more importantly, unbiased advice from someone who does this for a living."

"I thought Emilio was a financial advisor?" Grace was confused.

"Yes," Rebekah nodded, a look that reeked of 'duh' on her face. "Is that not what you need? Someone who can look at both of your businesses and see what room you have in your budget to hire people?"

"When you put it that way, I guess that's exactly what we need. Thanks, Rebekah," she hugged her friend, then exited the car feeling lighter than she had in weeks. There was light at the end of the tunnel, after all.

***

As predicted, Mayor Allen was too busy to play the role of the disapproving father. He did, however, have a few suggestions if and when Shelley's 'friends' fell through. That alone gave Grace the confidence to attend her eleven o'clock meeting.

When eleven thirty passed with no sign of Shelley, Grace's confidence faltered. "That woman is going to be the death of me," she announced to Jilly.

Jilly, who was busy cleaning the windows, looked over her shoulder at Grace. "She's just being dramatic," she said. "She's a star now, remember? Stars are known for keeping people waiting."

"How do you know that?" Grace asked suspiciously. She had been sitting in her chair scrolling through costume sites for what felt like forever, and she was beginning to get cranky.

"I can see her sitting on a bench across the street. It looks like she's talking to herself, but she's either on a call or recording a video.

Grace jumped out of her chair and rushed to the window to see what Jilly was referring to. "Huh," she said when she spotted Shelley. "You really think she's waiting to make a dramatic entrance? Or could she be waiting on those 'friends' she talked about?"

Jilly shrugged. "Either way, she's over there instead of in here."

"Should I go confront her?"

"I imagine that'd be about as productive as banging your head against the wall. That woman isn't going to do anything she doesn't want to do."

"Yeah, you're right. Probably best not to ruin whatever she has planned anyway," Grace said as she rolled her eyes.

She returned to her seat and continued scrolling through costume sites. None of them had the look she was after, and with the timeline dwindling, that was a big problem. Grace sighed and closed her laptop. Just once, it would be nice if something came together without issue.

"What's wrong?" asked Jilly. "Is Shelley really getting to you that badly?"

"No," Grace said absentmindedly. "I mean, yes, but she's not my only problem."

"Care to elaborate?"

"I can't find the costumes I'm looking for, and time is running out. We're already pushing it as it is; there's no way we could swing doing something custom."

Jilly finished the windows and took a seat across from Grace. "The costumes don't need to be as elaborate as you think. While it is true that they were decidedly more formal than we are today, the women would have been wearing traveling clothes, which were a lot more simple than, say, a ball gown. All you need to do is add a hoop to the right dress style, pick a complimentary shawl, and then do their hair in the correct style. Most of those items can be found at thrift stores."

"Really?" Grace asked in surprise. "What about the men?"

"Again, it all comes down to the accessories. If you want, once we know who the actors will be, I can go shopping with you and help you out?"

"I would love that!" Grace gushed. "Thank you so much!"

Jilly smiled, the first smile Grace had seen that reached her eyes. "It's no problem," she said humbly. "This kind of thing is right up my alley."

"You like making costumes?" Grace asked, genuinely curious.

"Quilting is more my style, but I won't turn down a chance to pick up a needle and thread."

"I need to introduce you to my granny," Grace said, the wheels in her head turning. She could start a sewing club. Then Granny wouldn't have to wait for a holiday to do something she seemed to love so much.

"I'm here," Shelley sang, interrupting Grace's thoughts.

Grace resisted the urge to make a snarky comeback and instead looked around for the friends Shelley was supposed to bring. "You seem to be missing a few people," she said, her brow raised. Okay, maybe she didn't resist hard enough.

"Oh, them," Shelley waved her hand dismissively. "None of them were able to match my acting skills, so I told them not to bother."

"Are you going to play all of the roles yourself?" Grace managed to ask with a straight face.

"You know, that's a great idea," Shelley said enthusiastically. "Just think of all the views I'd get!"

This was not going in the direction it needed to, and Grace was starting to panic.

"That's true," Jilly agreed. "But, the main job of a supporting cast is to prop up the star. If you played all the characters, you might not get the props you deserve."

Shelley appeared to give that some thought. "You're right," she finally agreed. She turned to look at Grace. "You need to find people who will make me look good."

It took every ounce of strength Grace had not to tell her that was impossible. Instead, she agreed to Shelley's demands, thankful she had anticipated this and was already a few steps ahead of her. "Of course," Grace said through gritted teeth.

Jilly pulled out a measuring tape and approached Shelley. "Grace, please write down Shelley's measurements as I read them out loud to you?"

"What's that for?" Shelley asked suspiciously.

"For your costume," Jilly explained.

"You already found a costume for me?" Shelley asked Grace. She held her arms out to her side as Jilly took measurements.

"We're putting together a custom costume for you," Jilly told her, alternating between speaking and calling out numbers.

"That better not be code for cheap," Shelley muttered.

"Trust me," Jilly said as she moved to measure her waist. "This costume is going to be one-of-a-kind."

Shelley didn't look convinced, but she let the subject drop for some reason. Now, all Grace had to do was convince the rest of her cast to agree to the job. Well, that, and find the accessories they needed to make the costumes. Piece of cake, right?

-Days till Halloween-

Eleven

To her immense surprise and delight, Cole agreed to meet with Emilio, so she immediately set up an appointment before he could change his mind. Not that she believed he wouldn't be interested in making changes; it's just, well, Cole was a creature of habit, and they tended to avoid change at all costs. The appointment was set for ten o'clock, giving them plenty of time to finish breakfast and head to the office.

"Hello again," Emilio greeted them. Only thirty minutes had passed since they'd all had breakfast together.

"Fancy meeting you here," Grace teased.

"I brought the paperwork you asked for," Cole said, handing him a folder with a mound of papers sticking out.

"Thanks," he replied as he accepted the folder. "I'll need some time to go over this in-depth before I can give you any real advice, but for now, why don't you guys give me an idea of what you're looking for."

He led them into the conference room, where they all took seats around the table. "Can I get you guys something to drink?"

They shook their heads, Grace reaching under the table to take Cole's hand. For some reason, he seemed nervous, which surprised her. "Um," she began, Cole's nervousness rubbing off on her. Did he really want to do this, or was he just humoring her?

"We would like you to look at our finances and see if we have room to hire an employee or two without risking our financial future," Cole explained. "I know you have an investment in the hotel, but I'm hoping that won't keep you from giving an unbiased opinion." Cole looked away, a sheepish expression on his face.

"There's no need to be embarrassed," Emilio assured him. "Your concerns are valid, but I can assure you I am a man of numbers. As long as the numbers won't put the hotel in the red, I see no reason not to consider hiring some help for Grace. After all, if we want to grow, she will need help anyway."

"I would appreciate the same consideration for the farm," Cole said.

"OH MY GOSH!!" Vanessa, Emilio's girlfriend, screamed as she rushed into the conference room.

"What's wrong?" Emilio asked, an alarmed look on his face.

"WE WON!!" she screamed again. She pulled on his arm until he stood up, then threw her arms around his neck as she jumped up and down.

Grace and Cole exchanged wide-eyed glances. They had known Vanessa as long as they'd known each other and had never seen her this excited about anything.

"Baby, calm down," Emilio said gently. "What did we win?" He looked into her eyes, a bewildered look on his face.

"We won the Halloween wedding package! We're getting married!" Vanessa was slightly more subdued on the last part, as if finally realizing her partner had no idea what she was talking about.

"We're getting what?" he asked.

"Maybe we should go," Grace began, standing up and collecting her purse.

"No, stay," Vanessa told them. "You can celebrate with us!"

Cole and Grace exchanged glances again, the awkwardness of the situation not lost on them. They resumed their seats and tried not to stare at the couple before them.

"Um, Vanessa, we're not even engaged," Emilio said. He tugged at the collar of his shirt with his finger as if trying to loosen a noose.

"I know, but we've talked about it at least a thousand times. All we're doing is moving the goalpost forward a bit," she replied, some of the excitement fading to hurt and concern. "You know how much weddings cost; I thought you'd be thrilled to have the wedding of our dreams for free."

"What do you mean, free?" he asked, still obviously freaked out yet curious at the same time.

"Haven't you heard about the promotion the radio station's been doing?" she asked incredulously. "They're giving away an entire wedding for free. As in, everything is paid for by someone other than us."

"I remember Rebekah mentioning something about it at breakfast one morning, but I wasn't really paying attention," he admitted.

"Figures," Vanessa said, rolling her eyes. "Look, I know this is sudden, but thousands of people entered that competition. The fact we won seems like a pretty big sign to me, don't you agree?"

Emilio looked like a deer caught in the headlights. Grace tried to think of a way to diffuse the situation, but her mind was drawing a blank. She would be horrified if Cole reacted like this to the idea of marrying her, but she couldn't imagine springing a last-minute wedding on him either. That was one of the things she had disliked about this promotion. It was very bold of the promoters to assume that everyone who entered was engaged and ready to get married in the span of ten days.

The phone rang, and Emilio quickly jumped at the chance to leave the room, promising to return as soon as he finished the call. As soon as he left, Vanessa sat in the chair he had just vacated and put her head in her hands.

"He doesn't want to marry me, does he?" she asked out loud.

"I think he's just surprised," Cole said gently. "That's a lot to spring on a man without warning."

"And if Grace had won?" she asked, her brow raised. "Would you have reacted the same way?"

Cole glanced at Grace before he replied. "I honestly don't know how I would respond. A sudden wedding like this would rob me of the chance to propose, would rob us of the opportunity to plan the wedding of *our* dreams. That would certainly make me hesitate."

Grace wasn't sure how to feel about his response. In theory, she agreed with him; in practice, she would have been just as upset as Vanessa. Relationships were complicated, and right now, she was very concerned about her friends and their ability to navigate these unprecedented waters. She just wished there was something she could do to help.

Although, now that she thought about it, she did have a vested interest in the outcome. If they didn't go through with the wedding, what would happen with the hotel and B&B? They had already canceled their plans for a Halloween Experience since both places were booked for the promotion. Would they still get paid if no one showed up?

Grace felt terrible for thinking about money at a time like this, but she couldn't afford not to think about it. There were a lot of people counting on the money this event was supposed to bring in. She was still trying to figure out how to broach the subject when Emilio returned.

"Vanessa, I really think you and I need to talk privately," he said, glancing at Cole and Grace. "Do you guys mind rescheduling this meeting for another day?"

"I believe you already have everything you need from us," Cole said as he got to his feet. "Just let us know when you're done with your analysis." He grabbed Grace's hand and led her out of the conference room. When they were safely outside, he stopped to look at Grace. "Please don't start getting ideas in that pretty little head of yours that I don't want to marry you," he drawled.

"Well?" she asked, crossing her arms over her chest.

"Well, what?" he asked, a confused look on his face. He adjusted his signature cowboy hat, lowering the rim to just above his eyes, making it hard for her to see them clearly.

"Do you?" she asked. "Want to marry me," she continued when he remained silent.

"Of course I do," he replied. "Look, Grace, what happened back there has no bearing on our relationship. Let's leave all that awkwardness to them," he said. "Please," he practically begged as she appeared unmoved.

Grace sighed and looked at her watch. It was almost time for Bea's Bakery to close, and if she hurried, she could catch Bea before she left for the day. "Okay," she said reluctantly. She wasn't sure why she was suddenly feeling so cranky. Was it some kind of female solidarity thing? Regardless, she needed to get going, so she stood on her tip-toes and kissed his cheek. "I'll see you later," she said.

Cole followed her down the sidewalk despite his truck being parked in the opposite direction. "Grace," he said, grabbing her arm and pulling her to him. "That is no way to say goodbye," he murmured against her lips.

She let out a small sigh as she kissed him back, eventually allowing herself to relax into him. This was much better than the chaste peck on the cheek she'd given him. Why was she even mad at him? As far as she was concerned, it no longer mattered.

A horn honked, causing them to break apart, though his eyes never left hers. "Will I see you tonight?" he asked.

"Of course," she replied. Even if she were still mad at him, nothing would keep her from spending what little precious time they had together.

He kissed her one last time, then turned toward his truck. "I'll see you later," he called over his shoulder.

"Later," she replied. Later couldn't come soon enough.

***

Grace made it to Bea's with one minute to spare, as Bea was just turning the open sign to closed when Grace pushed open the door. "Hey, stranger," Grace said to Bea. "Do you have a minute?"

"Sure," Bea replied. "What can I do for you?"

"I've been worried about you," Grace said. There was no time for small talk, so she cut to the chase.

"Worried about me? Why?"

"Because you're usually the first one on board with our crazy schemes, but lately, you've wanted nothing to do with them."

Bea surprised her by laughing. "It's nothing personal, dear," she replied. "I guess I'm just getting tired. I've been waking at four in the morning for decades, and it's losing its luster."

"Are you thinking about retiring?" Grace asked, a mixture of emotions hitting her all at once. Bea's Bakery had been a place of refuge for Grace since she was five. She could always count on Bea offering her a shoulder to cry on with tea and pastry. However, she couldn't fault her friend for wanting to slow down and do something new. Wasn't that the thing Grace was trying to get Cole to do? Well, something similar, anyway.

"I guess I am," Bea admitted hesitantly. "Or, at the very least, maybe going from open five days a week to three," Bea shrugged. "I don't know; I guess I'm trying to figure out what I want to do."

"I understand," Grace said, patting her on the back. And she did. She, too, felt like she was in some sort of transition phase, and it was both exciting and terrifying at the same time. There is comfort in the familiar, even when the familiar is no longer what one wants and needs.

"Hey, do you know anyone who might want to play the role of a disapproving father for the haunted hotel event we're putting on?" Grace asked. Mayor Allen had given a few suggestions, but none had panned out, and Grace was getting desperate.

"I bet Junior would," Bea laughed. "That kind of thing would be right up his alley!"

For some reason, asking Junior had never crossed her mind, though now that Bea mentioned him, Grace couldn't imagine anyone else in the role. "Thanks, Bea; I knew I could count on you!"

"Anytime, dear," she said with a smile.

"I better get going," Grace checked her watch again and saw it was well past lunchtime. Time sure did seem to fly by these days. "I promise not to bug you with any more crazy ideas," Grace promised.

Bea gave her a quick hug. "I love your crazy ideas," Bea reassured her. "I just may need a break once in a while, that's all."

Grace nodded and headed out the door. There was a solution to this problem; she just had to find it. A solution that didn't include losing the town's only bakery. For now, she had bigger fish to fry, and that started with a thorough look through the contract Molly signed with the radio station. Hopefully, their financial future wasn't dependent on her friends and their decision to make a life-long commitment on a whim.

-Days till Halloween-

Ten

"Have you heard the news?" Rebekah whispered to Grace as they made breakfast.

"Not only did I hear it, I was there," Grace whispered back. "And it was every bit as awkward as you're imagining."

Rebekah's eyes went wide as she looked at Grace in surprise. "You were there? And you didn't tell me?" she accused.

"I got distracted," Grace said defensively. After she left Bea's, she'd gone home to make lunch and found Jilly waiting for her. Or, more accurately, having a blast hanging out with Granny and Gladys. She had shown up with an armful of accessories she'd found at the local thrift shop and had been eager to show them to Grace. Of course, she showed them to the gals, which led them to team up to create far more elaborate costumes than Grace had planned. But who was she to get between an artist and her canvas? Or, in this case, a seamstress and her sewing machine.

"That's no excuse," Rebekah pouted. "You should have called me immediately."

She was right, but Grace had been dealing with a different distraction, one she had no desire to share with her friend. "I'm sorry," she said instead. "Did they cancel the wedding?" she asked curiously.

"Not yet, but from what I heard, it's not looking good," she said, shaking her head. "What was Vanessa thinking?"

"I have no idea," Grace replied, careful not to talk loud enough to be overheard. "It sounded like she entered on a whim with no intention of winning."

"I don't understand that kind of logic." Rebekah stirred the scrambled eggs, her aggressive movements turning them to mush.

Concerned for their breakfast, Grace gently grabbed the spoon and took over, giving Rebekah the job of buttering the toast. "I don't understand either, but it doesn't matter; what's done is done. Honestly, though, I have no idea what to hope for at this point. On the one hand, we need the money; on the other, I don't want my friends to rush into a marriage they're not ready for."

"I agree," Rebekah said, her agitation appearing to have subsided. "They have until five o'clock to either accept or decline, so now all we can do is wait and see."

"This is going to be a long day," Grace sighed.

They moved the platters of food to the counter and finished setting the table. "What do you have planned for the day?" Rebekah asked, her voice no longer a whisper.

"Cole is coming over to help me hang the new signs I painted," Grace said.

"That's exciting," Rebekah smiled. "Do things feel more official now that you've given the hotel and B&B proper names?"

Grace thought about it. "Yeah, I guess they do. It's always been in my mind that the B&B is just temporary, but now that we've named it, it has a much more permanent feel."

"I have a feeling seeing the new sign in the front yard will cement those feelings," Rebekah replied. "The same with the hotel; that poor thing has been empty for so long, it just blended into the background. Now it will look like a legitimate business again."

The voices in the foyer caught their attention, and they turned to see Cole and Riley step into the room. "Good morning, beautiful," Cole said, kissing her cheek.

"Good morning," she replied, hiding her face so they couldn't see her blush.

"Good morning, Riley," Rebekah said cheerfully, handing him a plate.

Granny and Gladys shuffled in, chatting excitedly as they pushed their walkers. "Good morning," they said in unison, both of them grinning ear to ear.

Cole, ever the gentleman, took turns helping them into a chair at the table, earning him an extra smile from the ladies. "What's got you two so happy this morning?" he asked them.

"We've been talking to Jilly, and we're thinking about starting a sewing club," Granny exclaimed happily.

"Not only that," Gladys told him. "We're working on the costumes for the haunted hotel. This is the most fun we've had in ages!"

Grace's heart practically beat out of her chest as Cole beamed at them, a twinkle of amusement in his vivid blue eyes. She didn't think it was possible to be any happier than she was now, with these people who meant more to her than life itself.

"I'm looking forward to seeing your creations come to life," he told them. "I think I have an idea for your first sewing club project," he said mysteriously.

"What's that?" asked Gladys.

"I'll let you know," he said, refusing to elaborate.

Grace was more than a little curious to know what he was thinking, but Cole was stubborn when he wanted to be, and right now, he wanted to be.

The conversation soon changed to Emilio and Vanessa's potential wedding, with Cole and Grace doing their best to avoid gossiping about the unfortunate event they'd witnessed the day before. The rest of the group pressed hard for details, but they stood firm in their decision not to violate Vanessa and Emilio's trust by sharing their very private business with others.

When breakfast was over, Cole, Riley, and Grace headed outside to install the first of the new signs. She was surprised when Cole pulled an adorable, freshly painted, hand-made, Victorian-style signpost out of the back of his truck.

"You made that for me?" she asked, her heart soaring at his thoughtfulness.

"What good is a sign without a proper place to hang it?" he grinned.

Grace threw her arms around his neck and kissed him. "Thank you," she whispered.

Cole pulled back so he could look her in the eye. "Anything for you, darlin'," he grinned. He looked around the yard. "Anywhere in particular you want to put the sign?"

"I was originally thinking we would have to hang it on the porch, but now that I have this beautiful signpost, how about in front of the lamppost by the flowers?"

"Sounds good to me," he replied. "I'll get the shovel and start digging while Riley gets the cement."

Twenty minutes later, the new sign was hung for all to see: the Enchanted Holiday Hideaway, now official.

"I love it," Grace said, clapping her hands in excitement. I can't wait for Granny to see it; she'll be so excited!"

One down, one to go. The three of them hopped in Cole's truck and drove to the hotel, where Cole surprised her with a different signpost. This one was black and made out of some metal he had bent and welded into a curved design.

"I was thinking we'd hang this one above the entrance," Cole said. "We'll have to drill holes in the brick, but that shouldn't be a problem."

"Sounds good to me," Grace replied, excited to see her sign above the door. It was all coming together; the Winter Haven Retreat was now officially open for business. Well, in limited capacity, of course.

This one took a little longer, but it still looked amazing when they were done. Some of her fellow business owners had come out to admire their work, each offering encouragement and congratulations on her new business. Now, all she had to do was sit back and wait to see what Emilio and Vanessa decided, which was far easier said than done.

***

Rebekah, Grace, and Cole gathered around the dining room table while waiting for the clock to strike five. The radio station had promised to call as soon as they had an answer, and the three of them were waiting with bated breath to find out what that was. Cole had very little riding on the outcome, but after witnessing the previous day's events, he felt just as invested as Grace and Rebekah.

"What do you think they'll decide?" Grace asked, her eyes never leaving the clock.

"I don't know them as well as you do," Rebekah said, her eyes glued to her phone as if she were willing it to ring. "However, if someone offered me my dream wedding for free, I'd be all over it."

"What if they offered it to you today?" Cole asked. "Would you marry Thorne after only dating for a couple of months? Would you expect him to marry you?"

Rebekah took a deep breath as she thought about Cole's question. "I guess not," she said thoughtfully. "He's a great guy, but we're definitely not at the 'til death do us part' phase. It would still be hard to turn the wedding down, though."

"So you think Vanessa and Emilio should turn down the wedding?" Grace asked Cole.

"I have no idea," he replied. "They've been dating a lot longer than a couple of months, but that doesn't mean they're at the 'til death do them part' phase either. What I do know is they shouldn't rush into something because of money."

"How many people entered the competition?" Grace asked Rebekah.

"They didn't give me that information," she replied. "If I had to guess, I'd say multiple thousands. Why?"

"Have either of you considered the possibility that this is fate? Out of thousands of people, Vanessa won; that has to count for something, doesn't it?"

Cole reached across the table and took her hand in his. "You, darlin', are a hopeless romantic," he teased.

Before Grace could respond, Rebekah's phone rang, startling her so much she dropped the phone she had been holding on the table. "This is it," she said, swiping the screen.

The room was so silent you could hear a pin drop as Cole and Grace waited to hear the news. Thankfully, the wait was short, as Rebekah was off the phone almost as soon as she answered.

"Well?" Grace asked impatiently.

"Vanessa said yes," Rebekah said, surprise written all over her face. She shook her head. "I honestly was not expecting that."

The doorbell rang, and the three exchanged looks as they wondered who it could be. "I'll get it," Cole said, rising to his feet. A minute later, he returned with Vanessa, who was sobbing into his shoulder. He looked at Grace, a helpless and somewhat desperate expression on his face.

Surprise momentarily kept her rooted to her chair before she leaped into action; Grace grabbed a tissue box while Rebekah made tea. Cole, for his part, managed to get Vanessa into a chair before he wandered off to 'check on Granny.'

Vanessa sobbed into her arms for a full five minutes before calming down long enough to talk. "I told
the radio station yes," she choked out, tears streaming
down her cheeks. "But Emilio said no."

A new round of sobs began as Grace and Rebekah
looked at each other helplessly. This was not at all what
they had been expecting. Rebekah placed a cup of tea
in front of Vanessa as she sat next to her, gently rubbing
her back.

The doorbell rang again; this time, Grace jumped up
to answer it. On the other side stood a miserable-look-
ing Emilio. "Are you looking for Vanessa?" Grace asked
him.

"No, why?" he asked cautiously.

"Because she's inside, and she's sobbing uncontrol-
lably."

Emilio pushed past her, sprinting into the house.
When he reached Vanessa, he knelt beside her, pulling
her into his arms. "Why are you crying?" he asked gently.

Grace, who had returned to the dining room, exchanged another glance with Rebekah. What on earth
was going on? From the way Vanessa was carrying on,
Grace had expected Emilio to run in the opposite direction, not rush to her side to comfort her.

"I called the radio station to tell them no," she
sobbed, her face buried in his shoulder, causing her
voice to come out muffled. "But when they answered
the phone, I blurted out 'yes' instead."

Emilio sighed as he began to rub her back in soothing
circles, much like Rebekah had just been doing. "You
really want this wedding, don't you?" he asked.

Vanessa nodded, too afraid to voice her feelings out loud. "Why didn't you tell me that?" he asked, his voice laced with hurt.

"Because I didn't want you to feel pressured to agree," she replied.

"Sweetheart, you should know by now that you can trust me. That includes trusting me enough to be honest with me and trusting me to be honest with you. I think we need to go and have another talk," he said, pulling her up to stand.

He looked around the room at his friends, a small smile on his lips. "We'll let you know how things turn out." He led Vanessa to the front door and quietly slipped through it while the rest of them were left speechless in the dining room.

"Well," Cole said, clearing his throat. "That was unexpected."

Grace looked toward the living room door where he now stood holding a sleeping Piper in his arms. "How long have you been standing there?" she asked him.

"Long enough," he shrugged.

"What do we do now?" Grace asked out loud. "I'm not sure I can handle another round of the waiting game."

"It doesn't look like we have a choice," Rebekah sighed. "I'll see you guys later," she said.

"Guess that leaves us," Grace said to Cole. "How about I make dinner while you find a movie to watch?"

"Sounds good to me," he replied.

Too wound up to cook something extravagant, she took some premade pasta sauce out of the freezer and put some noodles on to boil. As she stirred the sauce, she felt strong arms wrap around her waist.

"You should also know by now that you can trust me," Cole whispered against her ear.

"Who says I don't?" she asked, her free hand lacing with his.

"I don't know; it's a feeling I sometimes get. You were surprised when I said I wanted to have kids with you and surprised I was willing to meet with Emilio to discuss our future. Now that I think about it, you seem surprised every time I agree to do something for you. Why is that?" he asked softly as he trailed kisses down her face.

Grace turned into his embrace, holding on to him tightly. "I think a part of me has always been afraid to allow myself to believe in a future for us," she said quietly.

Cole leaned back to look at her, concern in his eyes. "Do you not want to be with me?" he asked.

"That's the only thing I want," she replied. "I'm just scared you'll leave me. Either because you finally realize you can do better, or because..." she trailed off, the words too painful to say.

"Because something happens to me," he finished for her.

Grace lowered her eyes and nodded. Losing him was her biggest fear. Even bigger than losing Granny. A part of her accepted that would happen at some point, though she still hoped that point would come much later, but losing him was a fear she felt deep in her bones to the core of her soul. Without Cole, life simply wouldn't exist anymore.

Cole pulled her close, his arms wrapping tightly around her. "I can't promise I won't leave this world before you," he murmured against her hair. "But I can promise I will love you every second of every day until that time comes.

It's all I have to offer you, baby girl. It's up to you whether or not you can accept it."

"I promise to love you, too," she whispered back. "It's not nearly enough," she said as she kissed his neck. "But it'll have to do."

- Days till Halloween-

Nine

Breakfast was just about over when Molly, Grant, and baby Eliza entered the dining room.

"Oh my gosh!" Grace exclaimed happily as she ran over to them. She hugged Molly and then bent down to see the baby sleeping peacefully in her carrier. "You're just the cutest thing in the world," she whispered to Eliza.

"How have you been?" asked Granny.

"Tired, but well," Molly said with a smile. "How have things been around here? I feel like it's been forever since I've seen all of you."

"Things are about the same," Grace replied. "Shelley is a nightmare; the wedding is in question, you know, the usual."

"Oh no, what's wrong with the wedding?" asked Molly.

Molly looked horrified, which was all the confirmation Grace needed they would not get paid if the wedding was canceled.

"Vanessa won, but she and Emilio are not even engaged, much less ready for a wedding," Grace explained.

"Can't the radio station just pick a new winner?" Grant asked.

That was a great question. One Grace should have thought of the other day. "I could have used your voice of reason a few days ago," Grace teased. "It never crossed my mind to suggest that."

"It's nice to know I've been missed," Grant grinned.

"Oh, you have both definitely been missed," Grace assured them. "As for now, I guess we'll just wait and see. Can I get you some breakfast?" she asked them.

"We already ate," Molly replied. "We just came by to see everyone and get out of the house for a while. It's been nice having time to recuperate, but I was starting to get cabin fever."

The baby started to fuss, so Molly picked her up and held her to her chest. "Would you like to hold her?" she asked Grace.

"I would love to!" Finally, the moment she had been waiting for had arrived. Grace sat down next to Molly and held out her arms so Molly could place the baby in them. Grace was surprised at how tiny and fragile Eliza felt in her arms. Surprised and a little scared that she might drop or hurt her somehow. "She's so tiny," Grace said to Molly, clearly uncomfortable.

"You're doing fine," Molly reassured her. "Before you know it, you'll feel like a pro. Now, what else is going on? How is the haunted hotel coming along?"

Grace rolled her eyes. "Shelley's being Shelley, but she's at least doing what she said she would, so that's something."

"Is there anything I can do to help?" asked Molly. "My body might need rest, but my mind is going crazy without a problem to solve."

"Yeah, you can tell me what to do about this," Rebekah said, showing Molly her phone.

Grace leaned over to see what Rebekah was talking about and sighed heavily when she saw the video was of Shelley. They watched in stunned silence as Shelley paced back and forth on the hotel roof in another one of her wedding dresses, this time crying out for her lost love and threatening to end it all if he didn't return to her. One could only hope she was in character, but with her, you never knew for sure.

"Is this live?" Grace asked Rebekah in concern. "Should we call the fire department or something?"

"I think she filmed it last night as some kind of promotion," Rebekah replied. "Regardless, she could have fallen off the roof."

That got Grant's attention, and he quickly came around to watch the video. "How did she get up there?" he asked incredulously.

"Someone's filming her," Grace pointed out.

"I'm not sure if that's better or worse," said Grant. "That is a serious liability issue; we must stop this immediately."

"Looks like we need to make sure no one else can access the roof," Grace told him. "Before we open the hotel again. Just imagine what could happen—"

"Say no more," Grant interrupted her. "I'll call the contractor and ask him to secure the door," he walked off, phone in hand, muttering about crazy stunts and lawsuits.

Eliza began to fuss again, so Grace handed her back to Molly. "Guess you'll have to solve the next problem," Grace said sheepishly.

"I'll settle for being kept in the loop," Molly replied. "By the way, thanks for all the meals you've been sending over. I'm pretty sure we wouldn't have survived without you."

"You're welcome," Grace smiled. "I don't deserve all the credit, though; Rebekah did her share of the cooking."

"I was happy to help," Rebekah replied, still glued to her phone. "These videos are crazy," she said absentmindedly. "If even half of Shelley's followers are real, we'll be swamped Friday night."

"You mean people are actually engaging with her?" asked Molly.

"Yeah," Rebekah looked at Molly in surprise. "Her videos have thousands of likes and hundreds of comments, tons of them claiming they'll be there on opening night to check it out."

"Is that not normal?" Grace asked.

"I would say it's very unusual for someone who doesn't have celebrity status," Molly explained. "The real question is: will they follow through?"

"Isn't the real question: what will we do if they do?" asked Grace. "The hotel can only hold so many people, and honestly, the haunted hotel event was only supposed to be a fun, local attraction. We are in no way prepared to host a large crowd. What will we do with them? The fair doesn't start until Sunday, and we open Friday."

"Take a deep breath," Molly said, touching Grace's arm. "Every problem has a solution; we just need to figure out what it is."

Was that really true? Grace wasn't so sure. She had managed to pull off what felt like the impossible in the past, but her luck couldn't hold forever. "Is it possible to get the fair people to set up a few days early," Grace asked Rebekah.

Rebekah shook her head. "They're booked up through Saturday night. We're already pushing it to get them here and set up before Sunday night."

"We could call some local vendors and see if they want to set up early," Molly suggested. "I can't see anyone turning down the chance to make money for two extra nights."

"That's a good idea," said Grace. "But is a quick tour through a haunted hotel and a couple of food trucks really enough to pacify a crowd?"

"We could increase the price of the tickets and include a hot dog and soda," Rebekah suggested. "That might make the event feel longer since they'll need time to eat."

Piper ran into the room and jumped on the table, curious to see the new addition to the family. As Grace watched her carefully sniff the baby, an idea began to form. "What about a movie in the park?" she asked. "We would have to set up multiple ones to deal with the time issue, but that would give people something to do."

"Are we still doing the hot dogs?" asked Rebekah.

"I don't know. Do you think that's necessary?" Grace asked. "If we send them to the park, someone there could sell hot dogs, pizza, popcorn, and ice cream. That would keep things simple on our end."

"Sounds like a good idea to me," said Molly. "The movies would need to be family-friendly, though. That doesn't exactly mesh well with the haunted hotel theme."

"What if we showed older Halloween movies?" asked Rebekah. "Like old Alfred Hitchcock or Vincent Price movies? They're still scary and would fit the theme, without all the blood, gore, and violence the newer movies are known for."

Molly and Grace looked at each other.

"That sounds like it could actually work," Grace mused. "What do you think?" she asked Molly.

"I think it sounds great," she replied enthusiastically. "Do you two have time to make all the arrangements?"

"We can take it before the town council tomorrow morning," said Grace. "If they agree, there are people we can reach out to who can make it happen."

"Awesome! Well, ladies, seeing you again was wonderful, but I think we're ready to head back home," Molly told them.

She looked tired, and Grace immediately felt bad for bringing her into their problems, even though she did ask. "Can I help?" she asked Molly.

"I think I can handle it," Molly replied. She stood up and placed Eliza back in her carrier. A few minutes later, the baby was securely strapped in with a blanket wrapped snugly around her little body. "I'll see you later," Molly called out as she picked up the carrier and headed for the door.

When she was gone, Grace looked at Rebekah. "What do we do now?"

"Now, we take a much-needed break. There will be plenty of time for work tomorrow."

"What are your plans for the day?" Grace asked.

"Thorne and I are going to an apple orchard a few towns over. You and Cole should come; it will be fun!"

It sounded fun, but Grace wasn't sure how to respond. Did Thorne and Rebekah really want to spend their free time on a double date? Or would they prefer to be alone? How did other people navigate these complicated waters? Or was Grace the one making them complicated?

"I'll talk to Cole," Grace said, sure he would know what to do.

"Talk to me about what?" he asked, walking into the kitchen.

"Thorne and I are going to an apple orchard, and I just invited you and Grace along," Rebekah explained.

Cole looked at Grace. "I already had plans for us, but it's up to you."

Grace took that as her cue to politely decline. "You guys have fun," Grace told Rebekah. "I think I'll just stick with whatever Cole has planned."

"Okay then, have fun!" Rebekah replied.

"You too," Grace said. She walked over to Cole and wrapped her arms around his waist, leaning her head against his chest. "Do we really have plans?" she asked him.

He wrapped his arms around her and kissed the top of her head. "Yes, unless you'd rather do something else?"

"No, I'm sure whatever you have planned is fine."

They walked hand-in-hand to his truck, him helping her in the passenger side. When he got in on his side, he kissed her before starting the truck and driving them out to the ranch. Once there, he led her to the side-by-side and they got in, his dog Max jumping in beside them.

Grace laughed as she pet the dog, who appeared as happy to see her as she was to see him. "Where are we going?" she asked Cole, hoping their plans for the day didn't include fixing a fence or herding cattle to another pasture.

"You'll see," Cole said mysteriously.

His answer did not instill a lot of confidence. At this point, she could only hope her cute outfit would withstand whatever he was about to throw at her. A few minutes later, he pulled into a clearing and stopped next to a copse of trees.

Grace looked around in awe of her surroundings. The field before her was full of color, a sea of beautiful white, lavender, and yellows. Next to it stood a little table and chairs set for two. "You were really going to let me change our plans for the day and miss out on this?" she asked incredulously.

Cole shrugged nervously. "I never actually asked you out for the day, so it seemed rude to impose if you had other plans."

Her mouth opened and closed a few times as she processed that statement. "Um, if you're going to plan a surprise, I think it's okay to impose," she told him.

"Is that so?" he leaned down and kissed her, laughing when Max shoved his wet nose between them. "Apparently, I'm not the only one who wants attention," he said, petting his loyal companion.

"Nope, not the only one," Grace said coyly.

Smiling, he pulled her out of the vehicle and over to the table, where they found a picnic basket and a portable radio waiting. "My lady," he said, helping her into a chair.

"It's really sweet of you to do this for me," she told him.

"We'll see if you still feel that way by the time we're through here," he replied somewhat ominously.

Concerned, Grace laid a hand on his arm to stop him from pulling items out of the basket. "What does that mean?" she asked. Last night, he'd promised to love her for eternity; today, he was acting like they were about to break up, and it was not sitting well with her.

"Nothing," he said nervously. "Just that, you might feel differently later."

"Why would I feel differently? Cole, what's going on?"

Cole pulled off his hat and ran a hand through his thick, dark hair. He sighed, then looked at her. "I had this all planned out in my head, but now that you're here, I'm unsure what to do."

"You're really scaring me right now," she said, her voice quivering. "Please," she pleaded with him, unsure what she was asking for.

He stood up, walked over to her side, and got down on one knee. Taking both of her hands in his, he looked into her eyes, his full of emotion. "Grace, I have loved you since the first moment you walked into my bar, and I will love you for every moment hereafter. Will you please be my wife?"

She had watched enough movies and television shows over the years to know how she was expected to behave. All those thoughts fled as she launched into his arms, knocking him over and landing on top of him in the dirt. She kissed him repeatedly as she said yes, not stopping until Max came bounding over and, thinking they were playing, began licking their faces. Even then, she refused to let him up, preferring to stay in his arms, even if his giant dog slobbered all over them.

"Now, I really can't believe you were going to let me cancel your plans," she said as she helped him up. "Are you sure you really want to marry me?" she narrowed her eyes as she searched his face.

He pulled a ring out of his pocket and slipped it on her finger in response. "I've never been more sure of anything in my life," he replied. He framed her face with his hands and kissed her gently. "Do you like the ring?" he asked hesitantly.

Grace glanced at it and nodded. It could have been a rubber band for all she cared; all that mattered was he wanted to marry her. Her dreams were coming true; she was going to marry her soulmate.

"It was my mom's ring," he explained. "If you don't like it..." he trailed off, some of his nervousness returning.

"I love it," Grace assured him quickly. "Now that I know, it's even more special."

He brought her hand to his lips and kissed it, his eyes never leaving hers. "Should we tell Granny?"

"Yes, but that can wait till later. Right now, I just want to be with you."

His sexy grin spread across his face. "As you wish, my lady."

-Days till Halloween-

Eight

C ole and Grace planned to gather all their friends for breakfast so they could announce their engagement at once. However, there was one person they wanted to tell privately, so they delayed the morning chores to ensure they could meet with her alone.

Grace felt like a naughty teenager sneaking through her house at such an early hour, but she knew Granny was up, and their cautiousness would pay off. "Good morning, Granny," Grace said, hugging her. She was still in bed, but the lights were on, and she appeared to be working on something she was trying to hide under a blanket.

"Good morning, you two," she replied, a twinkle in her eye.

"Wait," Grace said, eyeing Granny and Cole. "You already know, don't you?"

Cole cleared his throat. "I told Granny when I was here the other night," he explained. "I wanted her advice on how best to propose to you so I could make sure it was special."

Granny reached out and took Grace's hand. "Don't be upset, dear," she said.

"I'm not," Grace pouted. "I just thought we were going to surprise you, and now I'm the one surprised." She glared at Cole. "You could have told me she already knew."

"In my defense, she didn't know you said yes," he grinned.

Granny's face lit up. "That's wonderful," she said, clapping her hands together. "Does this mean I get to make your dress?" she asked hopefully.

"Of course," Grace replied. She wiped happy tears from her eyes. She still had to face the rest of the group, and she didn't want her face to be red and blotchy when she did it. "I better get started on breakfast; we're about to have a hungry crowd on our hands."

"I'll help," Cole replied, taking her hand and leading her to the kitchen.

They got the ingredients to make a large country-style breakfast of eggs, sausage, bacon, biscuits, gravy, and hash browns. At this point, Grace had been making breakfast for large groups of people for so long she didn't have to think about what she was doing; it had become as natural as brushing her hair or flossing her teeth. Speaking in front of large groups was another story that never got easier, even when the group in question were her friends.

"You seem nervous," Cole observed as he scrambled the eggs. "We don't have to do this, you know."

"I want to do this," she reassured him in case he referred to more than announcing their engagement. "I just hope we don't seem insensitive, given what Emilio and Vanessa are going through."

"I forgot about that," Cole admitted, somewhat sheepishly. "We could always postpone our announcement until after the holiday," he reached for her and pulled her into his arms. "If you think you can handle keeping a secret that long," he grinned.

Grace held up her hand and looked at her new ring. "Does that mean I have to take this off?" she frowned. "I don't think I'm willing to do that," she told him, a little concerned that he was even willing to consider it.

"Hey," he said, kissing the tip of her nose. "My commitment to you is not tied to that ring. Whether you wear it or not, you're still my fiance, and I still intend to be your husband."

"I know it's just—"

"Good morning," Rebekah called out as she entered the dining room. "Sure smells good in here." She stopped walking and looked at them, her eyes narrowing at the guilty looks on their faces. "Am I interrupting?" she asked suspiciously.

"Not at all," Grace replied. She stepped away from Cole and began to form biscuits from the dough she had been mixing, using it to hide her red cheeks from her friend.

"Grace?" Rebekah prodded. "What's going on?" She walked over to the bar and plopped down directly before her.

Grace looked helplessly at Cole, who smiled back, amused by Rebekah's inquisition.

"You might as well tell her," he shrugged. "She'll never forgive you if you don't."

"Tell me what?" Rebekah asked, looking back and forth between them. "Come on guys, one of you just spit it out already!"

Instead of telling her, Grace held her left hand out for Rebekah to see, laughing when she squealed like a little girl.

"Oh my gosh!" Rebekah jumped off the bar stool and ran around the counter to hug Grace. "This is so exciting! I'm going to plan the best wedding you've ever seen!"

"What's going on?" asked Evie as she and Jake entered the room. She saw them hugging and approached, squealing as she saw the ring. "Is that what I think it is?" she asked, joining their hug.

As more of their friends filed in, the group surrounding Grace grew as the women exclaimed over the ring while the men gathered off to the side, congratulating Cole and watching the women in amusement.

"Looks like the cat's out of the bag," Cole whispered as he returned to the kitchen to finish breakfast.

"Guess so," she replied, wiping tears from her cheeks. She had expected her friends to be happy for her, but not to that level of enthusiasm. "I'm just glad Emilio and Vanessa aren't here yet. I still think we should hold off on telling them."

"Tell us what?" asked Vanessa. She and Emilio entered the room and approached the counter.

"Um," Grace cleared her throat as the room grew silent. "Cole and I are engaged," she said softly.

"What? That's wonderful!" Vanessa exclaimed. "Why on earth would you want to keep that from us?"

"Well, it's just..." Grace trailed off, unsure of what to say. The last thing she wanted to do was bring attention to her friend's current troubles.

"Oh," Vanessa said, realization dawning on her. "You don't have to walk on eggshells around us, Grace," she replied. "I can be happy for you and still work through my own problems."

"Does that mean you haven't made a final decision yet?" Grace asked.

Vanessa sighed and looked around at all the curious faces. "Every time we think we've come to a decision, one of us changes our minds," she explained. "I know time is running out, but we just can't seem to agree."

"The wedding is supposed to be one week from to-morrow," Rebekah said gently. "I've been moving for-ward as if you said yes, but if we don't send out invita-tions soon, no one from your families will be there. It's already extremely last minute as it is."

"I know," Vanessa replied. "I'll make sure we have a final decision by the end of the day. No takebacks," she added as she looked at Emilio, who stood next to her as she talked.

Emilio nodded in agreement but otherwise remained silent. From what Grace could see, he appeared solemn and withdrawn, a far cry from his usual cheerful de-meanor. She was about to ask if he was okay when the doorbell rang. A quick glance around the room showed everyone she invited had already arrived. Curious about who it could be, she went to the door to find out.

Two women waited on the porch outside the door. One was on the short side with shoulder-length brown hair; the other was tall with long hair and looked sus-piciously like an older version of Vanessa.

"Hello," Grace said cautiously. "Can I help you?"

"Hello," the taller woman said curtly. "We're here for the wedding." She looked at Grace expectantly, and when there was no response, she continued. "According to the

sign in your front yard, this is supposed to be the Enchanted Holiday Hideaway, is it not?"

"Yes, it is," Grace replied. "May I ask who you are?" she
looked between the women while waiting for an answer.

"I'm Sasha, and this is my sister, Andrea," the taller
woman replied. "The mother and aunt of the bride, re-
spectively."

Grace shook her head to clear her surprise. Vanessa had
just confirmed a few minutes ago that no decision had
been made, so how did her mother know to show up here?
"I apologize," Grace finally replied. "I wasn't expecting
you so soon; please come in," she stepped back so they
could enter and followed them to the dining room.

The look on Vanessa's face when she saw her mother was
enough to confirm Grace's fears; things were about to get
messy.

"Mom," she said, a mixture of fear and relief on her face.
She ran to her mother, threw her arms around her neck,
and held her tight. "What are you doing here?" she asked,
her face buried in her shoulder.

"What do you mean?" her mom asked in confusion.
"We're here for the wedding."

"What?" Emilio practically shouted. He looked at
Vanessa. "You already invited people? Without telling
me?"

"It's not like that," Vanessa replied, a pleading note in
her voice.

"Then what is it like?" he asked.

"Maybe you guys would feel more comfortable talking
in the living room," Grace interrupted. "The rest of us
could take our breakfast outside, so you'll have plenty of
privacy."

Grace motioned to everyone else to follow her, but Emilio held up his hand.

"No, that won't be necessary," he said. "I think it's time we get it all out in the open. No more secrets, right Vanessa?"

Vanessa's face fell as her moment of reckoning arrived. "My mom was the first person I called after I got the news from the radio station that I'd won," Vanessa explained. "It wasn't some malicious act or way to manipulate you, Emilio; it's the same thing I would have done had you proposed."

"Shouldn't I have been the first person on your mind?" he asked.

"You're always the first person on my mind," Vanessa sighed. "I called her on my way to celebrate with you. It never crossed my mind you wouldn't be as happy as I was."

"What do you mean he's not happy?" Sasha asked. The look she gave Emilio would have sent a lesser man running for the hills. "Is there some reason you're not jumping at the chance to marry my daughter?" she asked, her brow raised. "Is she not good enough for you?"

"Mom, please," Vanessa pleaded. "This is my fault, not his."

"I'm confused," said Andrea. "Sasha and I traveled a long way to be here. Will there be a wedding or not?"

"No," Emilio exclaimed. "There's not going to be a wedding, or anything else for that matter; I'm done." He stomped out of the house, slamming the door behind him.

The room was so silent you could hear a pin drop. Grace glanced around and saw everyone staring at their feet, embarrassment coloring their cheeks. She was no stranger to guests causing scenes, but none had ever been this heart-breaking.

"Why don't I show you to your rooms?" Grace asked Sasha and Andrea.

They followed her into the foyer, Vanessa tagging along as she clung to her mother.

"What am I supposed to do now?" Vanessa whispered. She appeared in shock, her face pale and withdrawn, her eyes glassy and unfocused.

"Why don't we worry about that later," Grace replied gently. "Right now, you need to lie down. Once I get everyone settled, I'll bring up some tea and your favorite breakfast."

"I don't deserve your kindness," Vanessa replied, tears running down her cheeks.

"You deserve all the kindness in the world," Grace reassured her.

She led them upstairs and showed the three women to their rooms, thankful she had the foresight to prepare them last week. After promising to return shortly with refreshments, she left them to unpack and returned to the dining room.

"Is Vanessa okay," asked a concerned Molly.

Grace shook her head. "No, but hopefully, in time, she will be."

"Someone needs to check on Emilio," said Jake. "He's not the bad guy and is likely hurting just as much as Vanessa is."

"I agree," Grace replied. "I'll give him some time and see if he's willing to meet me somewhere to talk."

"Maybe I should be the one to talk to him," replied Grant. "After all, I work with him."

"I won't stop you," Grace shrugged. And she wouldn't. But that didn't mean she wouldn't still reach out to him herself. She was the one who had played matchmaker last Valentine's Day, so she felt invested in her friend's relationship, as well as a little responsible. If there was anything she could do to help, she was going to do it.

-Days till Halloween-

Seven

Rebekah and Grace had planned to meet with the town council the previous day, but none had been available despite the short time frame. Regardless, the meeting had been pushed back to this morning, and they were anxious to get it over with.

The meeting room looked much the same as it had the last time they were there, the chairs still in a circle, Mayor Allen still defying logic and appearing as the head of the group despite the circular shape.

"Ladies?" Mayor Allen addressed Grace and Rebekah. "What can we do for you?"

Grace cleared her throat. "We want to set up a movie-in-the-park night for Friday night."

"Okay," said Mr. Wilkins. "I don't see a problem with that, but any particular reason why?"

"We have reason to believe the Haunted Hotel event will be bigger than anticipated," Rebekah explained. "So we would like to offer a second event for people to attend, as well as invite some local vendors to set up a few days early."

Mayor Allen cleared his throat. "It's not that simple," he informed them. "Showings like that require licenses, and I'm not talking about ones from the town. You will need to approach an approved vendor, pay a licensing fee, and then rent and set up the required equipment. With less than four days to go, I'm not sure it's feasible."

"If you're going to go through the trouble," said Bea. "Why not do it Saturday night as well? If you expect a big crowd on Friday, won't you have the same problem Saturday?"

Grace looked at Rebekah. "I didn't think about that. What happens if we can't get the license in time?"

Rebekah looked at the others. "Does anyone have any ideas of what we could do instead?"

They collectively shook their heads, and Grace groaned.

"Guess we better hurry up and find someone," she said out loud.

"At the very least, do you all agree to the plan if we can find someone?" Rebekah asked the group.

Mayor Allen raised his hand. "All in favor, say aye?"

"Aye," said the crowd.

"Guess that answers that. Anything else we need to discuss?" he asked, his eyes searching the room. When no one replied, he stood up. "Thank you all for coming; call me if you need anything else."

Grace watched him go, curious about where he was always running off. Could there really be that many people he showed houses to? Or was there something else he did with his time? She may never know.

"We should ask Molly if she knows someone we can contact," Rebekah suggested to Grace. "If anyone can help us, it's probably her."

"Plus, it will give us an excuse to see baby Eliza again," Grace smiled.

As they left the building, Grace glanced across the street and saw Emilio's car parked in front of the office. She had tried to call and text him several times, but he had ignored them. Sensing an opportunity, she told Rebekah to go to Molly's without her and headed toward the office. Once inside, she found Emilio in his office.

"Grace," he said, looking up from his desk when she walked in. "Um, I haven't had a chance to run those numbers for you yet, but I promise to get started today."

"I appreciate that," Grace replied. "But I'm actually here to check on you. Are you okay?"

Emilio stared at her blankly for a moment and then looked away. "Honestly? I don't know," he replied sadly. "I waited all day for Vanessa to come home, but she never did."

"She's staying with me," Grace told him. "I'm not trying to make you feel worse, but she's so upset she called her work and asked for a leave of absence. Her mom and aunt have been trying to convince her to go home with them."

Emilio's eyes went wide. "But they live in Georgia; I'll never see her again!"

"You broke up with her, Emilio; isn't not seeing her again the point?"

"I didn't—" Emilo sighed and ran his hand through his hair. "I didn't really want to break up; I was just so confused and frustrated that I overreacted and said things I didn't mean," he shook his head and looked at her helplessly. "What do I do? I can't lose her."

Grace had never seen a man more lost and hopeless in her life. Her heart ached for him and Vanessa, who she knew was feeling the same. "The first thing you need to do is decide what you want. I don't think it's possible to go back to how things were at this point. If you don't want to get married next week, fine, but you need a plan moving forward."

"I just don't understand," he said. He put his face in his hands. "We've barely talked about marriage, yet suddenly, it's now or never. How did we get to this point?"

"When we first met Vanessa, she was trying to escape Valentine's Day because she was the only single one left in her friend group," Grace explained. "Even those in her new group of friends are getting married. I think it's something she's always wanted."

"But why does it have to be now?"

"I can't answer that," she shrugged. "Honestly, I think it's a matter of opportunity presenting itself and Vanessa deciding to take it."

Emilio smiled at that. "She has always been a bit impulsive. And a Halloween-themed wedding would be right up her alley."

Grace nodded. "Definitely."

She could see that he was processing the information, so she decided to remain silent and give him time to think. She sincerely hoped they could find a way to make things work and would do anything she could to make that happen. Luckily, she didn't have to wait long for him to decide.

"Would you be willing to help me with something?" he asked hopefully.

"Of course, just tell me what you need."

"Can you have Vanessa outside at five o'clock this evening?"

"Um, yes, I guess so. What should I tell her?"

"Whatever you have to say to get her out there," he replied. "Just try not to mention me unless you have to."

Grace nodded. "I can do that," she stood up and got ready to go. I'll see you at five.

Emilio gave her the first genuine smile since she'd arrived. "Thanks, Grace."

***

Grace and Rebekah had spent the afternoon calling vendors for the movie-in-the-park event they planned to put on. After hours spent waiting on hold, only to be told what they asked for was impossible on such short notice, they finally found a guy willing to help. Luckily, while they had to pay an extra fee for expedited service, it wasn't too crazy, and if they could sell half as many tickets as they did for the murder mystery dinner, they would still make a profit.

"We should contact the food vendors and see if any of them are willing to offer a package deal for movie night," Grace told Rebekah.

They were seated across from each other at the dining room table, a plate of pumpkin bread between them. "What do you mean?" Rebekah asked, looking up from her laptop.

"I mean, for a specific price, they get a movie ticket, a drink, a hot dog, or something similar. It will be easier to sell tickets if people know exactly how much they'll pay, especially those with children.

"That's a great idea," said Rebekah. "An incentive for the vendors would be guaranteed sales. If we could sell the tickets early, it would also give us an idea of how many people to expect."

"At least for around here," Grace said, nodding in agreement. "We won't know until the event starts if Shelley was able to draw a crowd." She looked at her watch and saw that it was almost five o'clock. "I need to get Vanessa outside. Is there any chance you can come up with a good enough reason to get her out of bed?"

Rebekah frowned. "Why do you need to get her outside?"

Grace leaned across the table and whispered. "Emilio asked me to. I don't know what he has planned. I know he'll be here at five, and it's my job to have her outside waiting."

"Hmm, well, we could try to get her to go for a walk," Rebekah suggested.

"I thought about that, but I'm afraid she'll just refuse," Grace replied.

"She'll probably refuse regardless. We'll just have to go up there and strong-arm her."

"There's that New York spirit I know and love," Grace teased.

"That 'New York spirit' has opened many doors over the years," Rebekah said sheepishly. "It's never let me down!"

"Let's hope it doesn't start now," Grace said seriously.

They walked upstairs and knocked on Vanessa's door. When no response came, they slowly opened the door, surprised by how dark it was despite the daylight outside. A quick peek showed the curtains drawn and a lump that could be Vanessa hiding under covers in the middle of the bed.

Grace turned on the light and pulled the covers off her friend. "I understand you're upset, but this seems a bit dramatic," Grace teased.

"You wouldn't feel that way if Cole broke up with you," Vanessa sniffled.

"Fair enough, but I'd like to think if that happened, my friends would rally around and support me, which is exactly what we're doing," Grace replied.

"I just want to be left alone," Vanessa said, pulling the covers back over her head.

"Too bad," Rebekah said, pulling them back off her. "It's time for you to get up, girlfriend. No man is worth this much wallowing."

"Oh yeah, how would you feel if—" Vanessa began.

Rebekah held up her hand. "I'm the wrong person to start that with. The man I spent my entire life planning to marry left me in the middle of the night without a backward glance. I lost my friends, family, home, everything I've ever known, and he hasn't had the decency to send so much as a 'how are you' text."

She grabbed Vanessa by the hand and yanked her into a sitting position. "Hunter may not have been my 'one true love,' but he was my best friend. It hurt like heck when he left, but I didn't spend a single day in bed. So, guess what? You're getting up, you're going outside, and you're getting some fresh air. No arguments."

"Is she always this bossy?" Vanessa asked Grace.

"You were here last Valentine's Day; what do you think?" Grace grinned.

They went downstairs, Vanessa grumbling about friends and their 'lack of compassion.' Grace and Rebekah avoided eye contact to avoid smiling too much and giving the surprise away. When they reached the front door, Grace opened it and practically shoved Vanessa through to make sure she was the first one out.

The first thing that greeted them was the song, 'Monster Mash,' playing on an old-style boombox stationed by the stairs. Next was Emilio, dressed like Frankenstein's monster with a large bouquet of purple and black roses in hand, dancing to said song.

"What in the world," exclaimed Vanessa, her hand going to her heart. She turned to look at Rebekah and Grace standing behind her. "Did you know about this?"

They nodded in unison, their eyes glued to the dancing Emilio. While it was true they had known about him showing up, they had no idea what he had planned and were just as surprised as Vanessa to see him like that.

Vanessa walked down the stairs and approached Emilio, who promptly stopped dancing and held out the flowers to her. "What are you doing here?" she asked, accepting the flowers.

"You never came home last night," he replied.

"After you broke up with me, I assumed I no longer had a home to go to," she said softly.

"I would give anything to take back what happened yesterday," he told her. "I'm so sorry; I was just so frustrated and upset."

"I understand," she said, tears falling down her cheeks. "I never should have entered that stupid contest without talking to you first. Or told my mom." She let out a small laugh that turned into a sob.

Emilio pulled her into his arms and held her tight. "It's okay," he reassured her.

"I don't know how you can say that—"

He put his finger to her lips, then held her hands in his. "Last night was the worst night of my life, but I'm thankful for it because it reminded me just how much I love and need you. Vanessa," he dropped down to one knee. "I never want to spend another night without you. Will you marry me?"

The door behind Grace opened and closed, Sasha and Andrea joining them on the porch.

"What's going on?" whispered Sasha.

"Emilio just proposed to Vanessa," Grace whispered back. Tears flowed down her cheeks as she watched her friends. She was almost as happy for them as she had been when Cole proposed to her.

"Are you sure?" asked Vanessa.

Emilio reached into his pocket and pulled out a ring with a large, purple stone. "Does this answer your question?" he grinned.

Vanessa nodded as she held out her hand. Once the ring was on her finger, she threw her arms around his neck and hugged him tight. "We can have a long engagement," she told him. "We don't have to do the Halloween wedding."

"And miss out on the wedding of your dreams? I don't think so," he replied.

"So the wedding's back on?" asked Andrea.

Emilio and Vanessa turned toward the porch, surprised to see they had an audience.

"Guess there's no need to make a big announcement," Vanessa teased.

Sasha crossed the distance between them and pulled them into a big hug. "Glad to see I don't have to hunt you down and make you pay for hurting my daughter," Sasha teased Emilio.

"I'm glad to see that, too," he grinned.

"Welcome to the family," she told him. "Looks like it's time to go dress shopping; we only have six days until the big day."

"Actually," Rebekah called out. "It's costume shopping. It's a themed wedding."

"I have to wear a costume to my only daughter's wedding?" Sasha raised a brow.

"No one said it had to be a scary costume," Rebekah shrugged. "You could always go as a princess or something similar."

"Yeah, mom," Vanessa said. "This is your opportunity to do something outrageous; no one will judge you for it!"

Sasha appeared to think about it. "I guess we'll see what we come up with. For now, I'm just glad to see you happy again."

Vanessa wrapped her arms around Emilio's torso. "Me too, mom. Me too."

-Days till Halloween-

Six

"The wedding is back on," Grace announced to Cole when he entered the barn where she worked.

He looked surprised. "When was it off?" he asked, concerned.

"Two days ago when Emilio dumped Vanessa right in front of you," Grace raised a brow.

"Oh," a look of relief crossed his face. "That wedding. I'm glad to hear it."

"What wedding did you think I was talking about?"

He answered her with a kiss, which she readily accepted. She looked up at him with narrowed eyes when they broke apart. "Did you think I was talking about our wedding?"

"Maybe," Cole shrugged. "I'm happy for our friends, but our wedding is the one on my mind, not theirs."

Grace wrapped her arms around his neck and pulled him close. "We haven't even set a date yet, silly."

"Maybe we should," he whispered against her lips.

The sound of Rebekah's custom ringtone went off, and Grace pulled away, groaning. "If Rebekah's calling me this early, something's wrong," Grace explained.

"Better answer it then," Cole replied.

"Hello," Grace said into the phone.

"Sorry to bother you, but we have a situation we need to deal with," Rebekah said, her words coming out in a rush.

"What's wrong?" Grace asked, images of Granny hurt or worse flashing through her head.

"It's Shelley," Rebekah said. "Can you meet me at the hotel?"

"The hotel?" Grace asked. "Do I even want to know?"

"No, you don't. Just get here, please."

"Okay, I'll be there in five minutes," Grace hung up and gave Cole a quick kiss. "Duty calls," she rolled her eyes.

"Shelley again, huh?" he asked as he walked her to her car.

"Isn't it always these days?"

"Do you need backup?" he teased.

"Probably, but don't let her latest stunt derail your day. I would much rather deal with this myself and have time to spend with you later."

Cole hugged her close one more time, then opened her door for her. "Call me if you need me," he told her. "And Grace," he said.

"Yes?"

"Let's make sure we finish this conversation, okay?"

Grace nodded as he shut the door for her. She was a little confused by his sudden urgency to set a date. It hadn't been long since he urged her to slow down and enjoy their time together without the constant need to rush ahead. He must know something she doesn't, though these days, that seemed to be the case regarding almost everyone.

Despite her attempts to stay on top of things, Grace had felt two steps behind since last July. Because of that, a lot of things fell through the cracks, with Molly and Rebekah often picking up the slack. She was hopeful things would calm down once Halloween was over, especially since they had all agreed to take Thanksgiving off this year.

When she reached the hotel, she was horrified, yet not surprised, to find Shelley perched on the ledge of one of the third-floor windows. A man Grace had never seen filmed her from the ground below while Rebekah argued with Officer Smith.

"What's going on?" Grace asked, interrupting their argument.

"*Officer* Smith, here, is refusing to do anything about this," Rebekah replied, waving her hand toward Shelley and the cameraman.

Officer Smith sighed. "That is not what I said," he turned to Grace with a pleading look. "I admit what Shelley is doing is dangerous and stupid, but it's not illegal."

"But she's trespassing," Grace protested. "Isn't that illegal?"

"She has a key," Officer Smith replied. "Not only that, she told me you allowed her to film her videos here. Said you hired her to work for you. Does any of that ring a bell?"

Grace covered her face with her hands and groaned. She had created a monster, well, encouraged one anyway. Shelley was already doing crazy things before Grace got involved.

"You're right," Grace admitted. "I hired her and gave her permission to film videos. I never expected her to do this, though I should have."

Rebekah crossed her arms over her chest. "So there's nothing we can do?" she asked. "What happens if that fool falls and injures herself, or worse?"

"I'm not a lawyer, but if it were me, I would get her to sign a liability waiver ASAP," he replied. "I don't know if that'll be enough to protect you, but it's something."

"Thank you, Officer," Grace said. "I guess we'll take it from here."

They all turned to watch Shelley, clad in one of her more 'outrageous' wedding dresses, declare that life without her love wasn't worth living and then throw herself out of the window. A collective gasp sounded from the crowd as they watched in horror at what was sure to be her last stunt.

As Grace moved to check on her, Shelley came running over to the cameraman. "Did you get it?" she asked, her eyes wild and excited.

The cameraman gave her a high-five. "I got it," he replied enthusiastically. "Man, this is going to get so many views!"

Shelley hugged him, then looked their way as if she were just noticing their presence. "What?" she asked.

"What do you mean what?" Grace asked incredulously. "You just jumped out of a third-story window. We thought you were..."

Shelley dared to giggle gleefully. "That's awesome!" she exclaimed. "If I fooled you, I'll surely fool everyone else."

When everyone continued to stare her down, she rolled her eyes. "There's a stack of mattresses piled below the window," she explained. "I'm not really trying to kill myself."

"What if you had missed the pile when you jumped?" asked Grace.

"Evan planned the whole thing out," Shelley replied, referring to her cameraman. "He's an expert at math and stuff, so I was never in danger."

Grace turned to Rebekah. "We better get that liability waiver."

"Agreed," Rebekah nodded.

***

Once Grant and Molly returned from taking Eliza to her wellness visit, Grace filled them in on Shelley's latest stunt and agreed to allow Grant to handle the liability issue. She hated to bother him while he was on paternity leave but had to admit he was more qualified in these matters. Plus, Shelley was far more likely to take him seriously.

With that bit of unpleasantness over, Grace could focus on the fun part of her job: shopping with Jilly. The plan included a trip to the city to scour every thrift, craft, and vintage store they could find for costumes, accessories, and props, and it sounded almost as much fun as her earlier trip to the dollar store for Halloween decorations.

They met at Grace's and agreed to take her car to save time and gas. As Grace drove, Jilly pulled out a list of stores and programmed the first one into the map app on her phone. They rode in silence for a bit, each lost in thought.

"Hey," Jilly said, breaking the silence. "What's the deal with the mayor?"

"What do you mean?" asked Grace.

Jilly shrugged yet appeared curious. "He ran into me outside the grocery store last night, and I mean, literally ran into me. He was moving so fast, he knocked me to the ground."

Grace was surprised to hear that. It was not unusual for him to move quickly, but he was usually more cautious and aware of his surroundings when he did so. "I'm sorry to hear that," she replied. "Are you okay?"

"Yeah, I was more embarrassed than hurt. I'm just curious why he's always in such a hurry."

"I've been wondering that as well, lately," Grace admitted. "I mean, he is a busy man. Three jobs is a lot for anyone, but he does seem more busy than I would think is warranted."

"Maybe he's just trying to avoid getting stuck in unwanted conversations," Jilly mused. "I imagine that would get old after a while."

"Maybe," Grace agreed absentmindedly. She certainly wouldn't blame him if that were the case. As the mayor and the local pastor, when people stopped to talk to him, it usually involved a complaint or problem. If she were honest, that would also wear on her pretty fast. Once someone dumped a problem on her, she felt obligated to solve it, whether or not it was her responsibility. Mayor Allen likely felt the same way, only multiply that by a hundred, given his profession.

"Grace?" Jilly said.

Grace shook her head to clear it. "Yes," she replied.

"You haven't heard a word I've said, have you?" Jilly laughed.

"You've been talking to me?" Grace asked in surprise.

"I asked when the guests would be checking in." The smile remained on her face, but there was a hint of concern as well.

"Sorry," Grace smiled back. "I was just thinking about everything going on right now," she lied. "We already have two guests at the B&B, and the rest are supposed to start arriving on Saturday. Although," she said hesitantly. "Since it took the bride and groom so long to decide to get married, I have no idea how many people to expect."

"I guess we'll take it one day at a time," she replied. "I hope at least a few people show up."

"Vanessa's mom and aunt are here, plus they have their local friends, so it won't be that bad," Grace reassured her. "They just might not have a lot of out-of-town friends or family members show up."

"That's not always a bad thing," Jilly muttered.

Grace wanted to ask about her comment, but they had arrived at the first store, and Jilly was already exiting the car. Hopefully, Grace will get another opportunity later, or maybe, for once, she should mind her own business.

They walked around the vintage store and found a lot of great finds, some affordable, some not so much. Luckily, the men were pretty easy to shop for. A couple of vests, top hats, and bow ties paired with suits they already owned, and they were in business. Jilly even managed to find a cane for Junior that Grace knew he would get a kick out of!

The women required a little more creativity. They found a hat that would work well for Katie's character, but it cost almost as much as the men's entire wardrobe, so they passed and continued to the next store. The next three were busts, but on the fourth try, they hit pay dirt. Jilly found, of all things, a wedding dress that, with a few modifications, would be perfect for Shelley. They also managed to find a simpler dress for Katie.

"Not bad for half a day's work," Grace said as they surveyed the treasures in her trunk.

"Now the real fun begins," Jilly smiled.

"You keep saying that!" Grace teased. "So what, to you, is the real fun?"

"Bringing it all together," she stated. "I love starting with a vision and then bringing it to life. There's no greater feeling," she said wistfully.

"I think you missed your calling," Grace said gently.

Jilly frowned. "It's difficult to imagine a more difficult and cutthroat industry to get into than the fashion industry. You can have all the skill in the world, but without a name and a fortune to back it, you might as well give up before you try. Unless, of course, you like having your heart stomped on."

"What about doing custom designs for people?" Grace asked, sure there had to be a way.

"How do I find those people?" she asked. "No one wants to pay for custom work from someone they don't know."

"Even on one of those online marketplaces?"

Jilly made a face. "Those places are a race to the bottom, everyone competing for the most sales with the lowest prices."

Grace tried to think of some other avenue but came up empty-handed. She had experienced some of what Jilly was talking about with her printables business, but since those were digital products, she could afford to take the hit occasionally. She couldn't imagine what it would be like if she sold physical products.

"It's okay, Grace," Jilly placed her hand on Grace's arm. "Not every problem has a solution, nor is it your job to find one."

"I know, it's just..." she trailed off.

"Hey, how about we grab a pumpkin-flavored drink before we go home? It'll be the perfect end to our perfect day!"

Nothing lifts the spirits quite like a pumpkin-spiced latte! Grace readily agreed and drove them over to the nearest coffee store. She was willing to let this latest problem go for now, but only until she had time to research. Would she ever learn to stay out of other people's business? Probably not!

-Days till Halloween-

Five

Breakfast was over, Granny and Gladys were busy sewing, the house was clean, and for once, Grace felt she could take a moment to relax. These moments were few and far between, so to make the most of them, she made herself a cup of tea, grabbed a book she'd wanted to read, and headed for the deck. It was a beautiful day outside, and given the time of year, it would likely be one of the last ones before the cold set in.

Just as she reached for the handle to the back door, Vanessa came rushing in the front door, plopped down at the dining room table, and promptly buried her head in her arms as she groaned.

"Of course," Grace thought to herself. With a small sigh, she turned around, set her book on the table by the door, and then proceeded to make another cup of tea for Vanessa before joining her at the table. "Want to tell me what's wrong?" Grace asked, placing the cup in front of her.

Vanessa looked up, saw the tea, and pulled it close, fidgeting with the cup as she spoke. "Emilio's parents aren't coming to the wedding," she replied sadly. "This is all my fault."

She looked so dejected Grace couldn't help but feel awful for her. "Did they give a reason why?" she asked.

"They said they aren't able to take off work on such short notice," Vanessa replied.

Now Grace understood. "I understand how disappointed you both must feel, but we were expecting this, remember?"

"Yeah, I know," she said, focusing intently on the cup. "But I expected distant relatives to say no, not our parents. How will Emilio feel knowing his parents won't be there on one of the biggest days of his life? How will his parents feel? They're going to hate me," she exclaimed.

Grace reached across the table and put her hand on Vanessa's. "I highly doubt they're going to hate you," she reassured her.

Vanessa looked into Grace's eyes. "His mom cried," she said quietly. "She was already distraught when Emilio left Texas to move here; now she's devastated. She kept going on and on about losing her baby," she shook her head.

"What if we set up a video call so they can watch the ceremony live?" Grace asked. "It's not as good as being here, but at least they can still be a part of it to some extent."

"That's not a bad idea," Vanessa perked up a little. "I'll run that by Emilio and see what he thinks. Thanks, Grace, you're a lifesaver!"

Grace chuckled at the compliment. "Glad I can help. How is dress shopping going?"

Vanessa rolled her eyes. "My aunt found a costume she was happy with within five minutes of our first shopping trip. On the other hand, my mom wasn't happy with anything. We're supposed to go shopping again this afternoon. If she doesn't find something today, she will be out of luck."

"Have you tried taking her to the vintage shop?" Grace asked.

"No, why?"

"They have a lot of great options to choose from, and while I don't know your mom that well, this kind of place is right up her alley.

"Couldn't hurt to try," Vanessa shrugged. She stood up to leave, looking far calmer and more collected than when she had first arrived. "Thanks again," she said. "I don't know what I'd do without you!"

"Anytime," Grace pulled out her phone and opened it to her text messages. "I'll text you the name and address of the store. Let me know if you strike out there, and we'll come up with something else."

Once Vanessa left, Grace checked her watch; she still had time before her afternoon meeting with Cole and Emilio. After a quick stop in the kitchen to refill her tea, she grabbed her book and, once again, headed for the back deck.

"Grace!" Molly exclaimed as she rushed into the dining room, Eliza in tow. "I'm so glad you're here; I need your help."

So much for her relaxation time, she put her book back down and returned to the dining room table. "What can I do for you?" she asked Molly.

"I hate to ask this," Molly replied. "But I need to go to a doctor's appointment, and Grant isn't back from work yet. Is there any way you can watch Eliza for me?"

"I thought Grant was on paternity leave?" Grace asked.

"He is, but there was an emergency with one of their biggest clients, and he needed to deal with it. It's important that he still has a business to return to once his paternity leave ends," she explained.

Grace thought Molly sounded slightly defensive, so she decided to just go with it. "I'd be happy to watch the baby," she replied. "Do you have a list of instructions for me?" Knowing Molly, she would absolutely have a thorough list of instructions.

With a sigh of relief, Molly set the baby carrier and the diaper bag on the table. "The list is in the side pocket. She's already been changed and fed, so hopefully, she'll sleep the whole time I'm gone. If you need anything, Gladys should be able to help you."

"Sounds good," Grace replied. "Do you know how long you'll be gone?"

"Hopefully, no longer than three hours," Molly replied. She grabbed her purse, kissed Eliza goodbye, and turned to leave. "Thanks, Grace!"

Once she was gone, Grace walked around the table and looked at the sleeping baby. There was still time to attempt to read her book, but only if Eliza stayed asleep. Given her luck thus far, Grace would not hold her breath; however, she might as well try.

She picked up the carrier, grabbed her book, and reached for the door handle just as Eliza let out a wail loud enough to wake the dead. Grace looked heavenward momentarily, put the book back down, then turned toward Granny's room. She'd get a break someday, but today was not that day.

***

It was almost time for the meeting with Emilio, and Molly was still an hour from home. Left with no choice, Grace grabbed the stroller from Gladys's house, packed up Eliza, and walked down to the office with her. As much as she loved her goddaughter, her nerves were worn thin. Eliza had been fussing off and on since that first wail, and Grace had zero idea how to make her stop. Luckily, the walk calmed her down. They would have been out walking hours ago if Grace had known that would work.

She'd always been torn on her feelings toward having kids. A part of her wanted a large family with lots of kids so they'd have plenty of built-in friends and playmates. The other part was adamantly opposed to bringing children into the world. Losing her parents at such a young age had shown her there were no guarantees in life. It went without saying while Grace was incredibly fortunate Granny took her in and raised her, Granny was in no position to do that with any children Grace might have. With no other family besides Granny, having kids felt like walking a tightrope without a safety net.

Right now, though, as she stared into the stroller at Eliza's sweet little face, all bundled up and sleeping peacefully, she couldn't help but imagine what it would be like if she were her baby with Cole. Ten minutes ago, it was a very different story.

Grace saw Cole's truck parked in front as they approached the office. He had offered to pick her up, but since she could not safely secure the baby, she declined. He then offered to walk with her, but she had been so frazzled and stressed out she declined that, too. Now, she wished she had taken him up on his offer. The day was beautiful, the sky clear, the leaves a mixture of yellow, orange, and red. It was such a romantic time of year.

Once inside, she found Emilio and Cole in the conference room. Grant was nowhere to be seen, but since his office was in the back, he could be there, and she'd never know. Which was just as well; if Grant was still working, he was unlikely to take the baby anyway.

She pushed the stroller into the conference room and sat beside Cole, stopping momentarily to hug him. Unfortunately, when the stroller stopped, Eliza began to fuss. But this time, Grace was prepared, quickly putting her foot on the bottom of the stroller and rocking it back and forth to mimic walking. She smiled at Emilio. "We should probably make this quick," she motioned toward the stroller.

"I'll do my best," Emilio replied. He appeared uncomfortable but pushed a folder across the table to each of them. "I have gone over your respective portfolios and have some recommendations," he began.

Eliza took that as her cue and wailed again.

"I don't understand," Grace said, picking her up. "She's been like this ever since Molly dropped her off. Her diaper is dry, she refuses to eat, she doesn't want to be held..." Grace trailed off, unsure of what else to say.

"Here, let me try," Cole said, reaching for the baby.

Grace carefully handed her over, surprised when she stopped fussing and went back to sleep, safely nestled in Cole's arms. "Where were you a couple of hours ago?" she asked Cole, more than a little irritated at his effortless ability to calm the baby.

"A phone call away," he grinned. "Babies can sense stress," he explained. "When you calm down, she calms down."

Grace should have tried to read that book after all. With a nod, she turned back to Emilio. "Please tell me we can hire people," she pleaded. "That's the number one thing I want to know."

Emilio sighed. "It's not that simple," he replied. "If you take a look at your portfolio, you'll see—"

"Please make it that simple," Grace said, cutting him off. "I've spent the last few hours getting screamed at by a two-week-old; I don't have the mental bandwidth to discuss, much less understand, a bunch of graphs and charts."

Emilio sighed a second time, much more dramatically this time. "Fine," he replied. "The answer is yes, but there are caveats," he quickly added.

Grace turned to Cole, grinning from ear to ear. "Do you hear that? We might actually get to take a day off occasionally!"

"Hopefully, more than one," he said, returning her grin.

There was a time when Grace thought the sweetest thing in the world was a man cuddling with a puppy. But she had been wrong; it was a man cradling a baby. The sight of Cole holding Eliza, grinning his signature grin, took her breath away. Completely mesmerized, she forgot Emilio was there until he loudly cleared his throat, bringing her back to the present.

"Sorry," Grace said, looking away in embarrassment. "What were you saying?"

"I was saying there are caveats," he repeated. "We need to discuss your goals before we can make concrete decisions about the future." He looked between the two of them.

"But I guess we can save this conversation for another day," he laughed.

"Sorry," Grace said again. "It's hard to concentrate."

"I understand," he nodded. "We can try again after the wedding is over and things have settled down. Sound good?"

Cole and Grace nodded in unison.

"Great! In that case, I will let you two go on with your day," he gathered his papers and stood up. "Go ahead and take those folders with you," he instructed. "You can look them over when you get a chance; if you have any questions, you know where to find me."

"Thanks, Emilio," said Grace.

"Yeah, thanks," Cole said. He stood up, careful not to disturb the baby, and waited for Grace to push the stroller out into the hallway and out of the way. Once there was more space, he shook Emilio's hand. "I hope you don't feel like we wasted your time," he said apologetically.

"Not at all," Emilio shook his head. "Things have certainly been...interesting lately. I'm sure they'll settle down and return to normal soon."

"I'm sure you're right," Cole replied. He looked at Grace, an uncertain look on his face. "Well, we'll see you later," he told Emilio.

Grace led the way out the door, holding it open for Cole and Eliza. "What do you think he meant by that?" Grace asked once they were safely out of earshot.

Cole shrugged. "I suppose he was referring to the wedding. Unless we're missing something?" he raised a brow as he looked at her expectantly.

"I don't know," Grace said, equally confused. "I guess we'll find out."

They walked silently, Cole cradling Eliza while Grace pushed the empty stroller. Once they reached the house, since Molly still wasn't home, they continued up the street and over to the park.

"We still need to set a date," Cole said as he sat on one of the benches.

Grace sat next to him, careful not to bump him and disturb Eliza. "Are you sure you want to do that so soon?" she asked. "You're the one who claimed we're moving too fast."

"I've changed my mind," he said, refusing to meet her eyes.

"Okay, but why?"

"Why are you suddenly wanting to take things slow?" he asked.

That was a good question. It wasn't that she wanted to take things slow; she would march down to town hall and have Mayor Allen marry them this instant. It was more that she was curious and a little suspicious of his sudden change of heart.

"Okay, fine, how about two weeks from Saturday?" Grace threw out.

Cole was silent for a minute. "That would work," he replied.

"Are you serious?" Grace asked incredulously. She stood in front of him and forced him to look at her. "Alright, mister, you better tell me what's going on right now."

"Why do you assume something's going on?" he asked innocently.

Grace crossed her arms and raised her brow. "If something is wrong, I have a right to know," she said quietly.

Cole sighed and looked away again. "Nothing's wrong," he said. "It's just both of our parents are gone, neither of us has any siblings or extended family, except Granny, and she's in poor health. I just want to make sure we don't waste too much time and miss our opportunity to have our few remaining loved ones at our wedding."

Moved by his words, she walked around the bench and carefully wrapped her arms around his shoulders from behind. "I love you for that," she said softly. "And I would love to have Granny and Gladys at our wedding. But they would be so upset if they knew you were rushing things because of them. Especially since Granny wants to make my dress. We have to give her enough time to do that."

"How much time do you think she'll need?" he asked, leaning his head back against her.

"I have no idea," she answered. She kissed his temple as she hugged him close. "Why don't we talk to her later and then go from there?"

"Sounds good to me," he replied.

Grace smiled. "Good, now that that's settled, we should head home. Molly should be back by now, and I imagine it's getting close to feeding time."

As they followed the path, Grace thought about what Cole had said. The family they'd created, in a way, made up for the family they'd lost, but the hole their loss had created had never fully healed. Cole was right; they needed to take advantage of the time they had left with Granny and Gladys. Which meant there was at least one more wedding to plan before the year was out.

-Days till Halloween-

Four

"Mike from Mike's Movies and Music will be here in about an hour," Rebekah announced as she entered the kitchen. "Do you need anything before I meet him at the park?"

Grace looked at her watch and saw it was only eight o'clock. "Isn't it a little early for that?" she asked.

Rebekah shrugged. "He has to set up three movie screens, the projectors, and all the audio and speaker equipment. Plus, it sounded like he's a company of one, so I imagine it will take some time."

"Well, better to have it done early than late," Grace replied. "We've got things under control here, so don't worry about us."

"Is Jilly still coming by to help with the cleaning this morning?" Rebekah grabbed a piece of toast to butter while Grace finished the eggs.

"She should be here after she drops the kids off at preschool," said Grace as she scooped the last of the eggs out of the pan and into a warming dish.

It was almost time for everyone to arrive for break-fast, and thankfully, she was ready for them despite her late start that morning. Today was set to be a long day, with last-minute cleaning and preparations for the guests taking up most of the morning hours, then last-minute costume preparations for the haunted hotel in the afternoon, and then the events themselves. It would likely be midnight before she saw her bed again, an exhausting thought if there ever was one.

Jilly arrived as promised; her extra set of hands mak-ing short work of the cleaning upstairs. She had only been helping for a week, but Grace already felt she couldn't live without her. There had to be a way to keep Jilly; she just needed to figure out what it was.

After they finished cleaning, they began the prep work for tonight's dinner. Rebekah and Grace were the only ones who would be out that night, leaving many people still needing food. Since she needed to keep things simple and make sure there were extras, just in case, she opted for a couple of large crock pots full of beef stew, cornbread, and pumpkin pie for dessert.

"I can make the pies," Jilly volunteered.

"I will gladly let you," Grace replied. She loved pumpkin pie but needed help to keep it from coming out undercooked. No one likes undercooked pie.

They made small talk while they worked, Jilly telling stories about her kids and the new friends they were making.

"It sounds like they're adjusting well," Grace said cau-tiously. It was a difficult conversation to navigate, and despite her personal experience with losing her parents, she wasn't exactly sure what to say that wouldn't sound insensitive.

Jilly nodded as she rolled out the pie crust. "I know this sounds horrible, but my husband worked so much the kids barely saw him. They know Daddy isn't coming home, but for them, life isn't much different than it was before he passed. It's been much easier on them than on me, which I'm thankful for," she added quickly.

Grace placed a comforting hand on her arm. "I'm sorry; I can only imagine how hard things are for you."

"That's just it," Jilly looked up with tears in her eyes. "The hard part is that it's not hard. You look exactly how I feel," she laughed when she saw the look of confusion on Grace's face. "It's just I had already gotten used to being a single parent. The main difference now is I know for sure he won't be home for dinner. That's a terrible thing to say, isn't it?" she put her hand over her mouth, horrified by her words.

"I don't think it's terrible at all," Grace said gently. "I think you're still trying to process your grief."

"I was considering a divorce," she said quietly. "He had become consumed by his work. It was all he did. Even at home, he would lock himself in his office and work. On the rare occasion he would come out and join the family, he spent all his time talking to us about work. It wasn't always like that," she shook her head, the memories too painful.

Grace wasn't sure what to say. Cole worked a lot, too, but did everything he could to ensure they spent at least some time together. No matter how busy he was, he would drop everything and rush to her side if she needed him. What could she say to someone who had experienced the opposite?

"I don't know what to say," Grace admitted. "But I'll say this: you have nothing to be ashamed of. You're doing your best, and that's all anyone can ask or expect. So please stop beating yourself up; you don't deserve it."

Jilly thought about it for a moment. "Thanks, Grace, I really appreciate it."

"Anytime," Grace replied. "And I mean that. If you ever need to talk, I'm willing to listen."

Jilly smiled, and they returned to work, Grace chopping vegetables for the stews, Jilly preparing the pie filling. When they'd finished those tasks, it was time for a quick lunch of sandwiches and chips and then on to the costume fittings. Yeah, it was going to be a long day.

***

Leave it to Shelley to arrive two hours late. As the show's star, her costume was the most important and took the most time to create. If they didn't hurry, they would be late for the event. As if that weren't bad enough, Shelley's entourage had multiplied, each new addition more annoying than the last.

At first, it had just been Evan, the cameraman. Now she had a makeup artist, hair stylist, social media 'expert,' and some kind of personal assistant whose only job, as far as Grace could tell, was to keep a steady supply of drinks on hand for when Shelley demanded one. And because she was a diva of the highest order, she could only drink out of a bottle once; the soda was no longer fizzy enough after it had been opened. Grace wanted to give her a lecture on wastefulness but decided to save her breath; unless her lecture contained enough 'buzz words,' it would go over her head anyway.

Seeing the young assistant rolling around an ice chest full of soda was slightly amusing, though Grace couldn't help but feel sorry for her. What could have gone wrong in this woman's life to think following Shelley, of all people, around and waiting on her hand and foot was a good life decision? Or career decision?

Grace shook her head and did her best to keep the groupies out of Granny's room, where Granny, Gladys, and Jilly were working. Not an easy task when they all claimed a need to be by Shelley's side. It was like herding cats, though Grace strongly expected that would be easier.

The event was supposed to start at six, just after dark. Rebekah checked in around five to report the crowd in front of the hotel had grown so large the town had been forced to shut down the street. It appeared that Shelley's theatrics had worked, only now they had a new concern. Instead of not enough people showing up, they had way more than they had time to serve.

"What do we do?" asked Rebekah, her tone suggesting she was on the verge of panic.

Grace thought about it for a minute. "How long are the movies?"

"I don't know," Rebekah replied, confused. "About an hour and a half, I think?"

"How many people can we get in and out of the hotel in an hour and a half?" Grace asked. She got out a notepad and a pen and began to write down numbers. The movie times were staggered to accommodate the hotel schedule, so she would use that to their advantage.

"I believe we can get roughly one hundred and fifty in and out in that time," said Rebekah. "But Grace, it looks like there's around five hundred people here. Maybe more."

Okay, that complicated things. At that rate, accommodating everyone would take ten hours, and they did not have that time. Six hours were doable, but that wasn't enough time.

"I have an idea. Can I call you back in a few minutes?"

Rebekah sighed. "Yes, but please hurry."

Jilly walked in as Grace hung up the phone. "Everything okay?" she asked.

"Um, I don't know. How hard would it be to come up with another costume?"

"How long do I have?"

Grace looked at her watch. "Thirty minutes," she said.

"What kind of costume are we talking about?"

"One for when Ms. Hathaway meets the group on the train station platform?"

Jilly thought for a minute, then nodded. "Yeah, I think we could pull something together. Why?"

"I'll have to explain later; you get the costume; I'll get the woman I hope is going to wear it," Grace walked off, her phone to her ear.

"Grace, what's up?" asked Evie.

"Hey, you know how you owe me a huge favor for getting your sister out of your hair?" Grace asked. It wasn't entirely true, but desperate times called for desperate measures, and these were desperate times.

"Um, yeah," Evie said cautiously. "What has she done now?" she sighed.

"It's not that; I need a favor," Grace told her. When the line stayed silent, Grace continued. "Way more people showed up than we can accommodate, and I need to split the event in two. This means I need someone who resembles Shelley to play Ms. Hathaway before she becomes a ghost."

"I don't know, Grace. I'm not cut out for that kind of thing," Evie said.

"Look, all you have to do is stand by the railroad tracks and wait for your beau to show up. When he leaves, turn and run into the hotel, Shelley will handle the dramatic part. Plus, you'll get to wear a cool costume," Grace told her, emphasizing the cool part.

"How long do I have?" Evie asked.

"The event starts at six, so I need you here ASAP. Jilly will handle your costume, and I'll escort you as close as possible to the hotel. If it helps, I promised Shelley five percent of the ticket sales, and I'll give you the same deal."

"Okay, fine. I'll be there in five minutes, but you owe me now," said Evie.

"Some day we'll be even," Grace teased.

"But not today," Evie laughed.

They hung up, and Grace called Rebekah to explain the plan. "Here's what we'll do," Grace said. "You sell tickets in groups of three that coordinate with the movie times. Then, we'll split the groups up and rotate them in and out of the hotel. Evie will play Ms. Hathaway at the train station while Shelley will haunt the hotel. This way, we can do two groups at once."

Rebekah was silent so long Grace had to check her phone to make sure they hadn't disconnected. Eventually, she spoke.

"I think that will actually work," Rebekah said slowly. "Thorne's here, so I'll have him help me with the ticket sales. Just please, please don't be late," she pleaded.

"We'll do our best. Thanks, Rebekah!"

Evie appeared red-faced and out of breath. "There's cars," she panted, "everywhere. I had to run," she explained.

Jilly came out of the room, looked at Evie, and rushed her back inside, barking at Shelley's assistant to get Evie a bottle of water. Twenty minutes later, everyone was dressed and ready to go. Now, they just had to get there.

"The limo is here," Evan announced.

"What?" asked Grace.

"You didn't think I was going to walk there, did you?" asked Shelley.

"No, but how is a limo going to make it if a small car can't?" asked Grace.

Shelley rolled her eyes. "You obviously have no idea how limos work. When one appears, the crowd parts. You'll see."

Grace wanted to argue, but there wasn't time for that, so she followed the group and got in, thankful Shelley was in a generous mood. Or it was a 'told-you-so' mood. Either way, Grace secretly hoped Shelley was right, though she knew she'd never live it down.

Sure enough, the crowd parted the moment the limo turned onto the street. The street that was supposed to be blocked off. However, to Grace's surprise, when Officer Smith saw them, he waved them through. If a limo was all it took to receive this kind of treatment, she was surprised more people didn't hire them. Just imagine the kind of respect you'd get at an event with long lines.

The event started at six o'clock on the dot; Evie nervously making her big acting debut. Despite her earlier protestations, she was a natural, just like her older sister. By the time midnight rolled around, not a soul remained. They had done it; their first official event at the hotel had been a huge success. Now, they had to do it again the next night.

-Days till Halloween-

Three

Despite the late night, Grace still had to get up at the crack of dawn to do chores and make breakfast. At this point, she was counting down the days until this was over, and she could sleep again. If she were honest, she would still have to get up early, but at least she could go to bed at a decent time. She had never understood the people who bragged about their lack of sleep like it was some kind of badge of honor.

To her surprise, Rebekah joined her in the kitchen.

"I didn't expect to see you for at least another hour," Grace told her as she handed her a cup of coffee.

Rebekah groaned. "I was rudely awakened by the bakery owner who's supposed to make the wedding cake," she replied. "It turns out they received a surprise inspection from the health inspector yesterday and failed. They've been shut down for at least two weeks."

"Are you serious?" Grace asked, surprised. "What do we do now?" she asked when Rebekah nodded.

"Any chance you can make a wedding cake?" Rebekah asked hopefully.

Grace stopped chopping fruit and stared at Rebekah. "Surely I'm not your only option?"

"I'm afraid you are," she replied. "It's too short notice; no one else will even consider it."

Jilly walked into the room, looked at their faces, and backed up a step. "Is this a bad time?" she asked.

"No," Grace said as she poured another cup of coffee and held it toward Jilly.

Rebekah explained the situation to Jilly. "You don't happen to know how to bake a wedding cake, do you?" she asked.

"How big are we talking?" Jilly asked.

"It needs to feed around one hundred people," Rebekah replied.

"Would simple work, or does it need to be elaborate?" Jilly pulled out her phone and began to swipe at the screen. At one point, she paused and turned the phone toward Rebekah and Grace. "I could probably do something like this in four days," she said, showing them a simple, three-tiered cake with flowers.

"Could you make it black with purple flowers?" asked Rebekah.

"I don't see why not," Jilly shrugged. "What about the inside?"

"What do you mean?"

Grace turned to Rebekah. "What flavor, silly," she teased.

"Oh yeah, I forgot about that," she said, then appeared to think about it for a minute. "Honestly, I'm not sure we can afford to be picky at this point, so I'll leave that up to you." Rebekah went around the counter and hugged her. "Thank you so much; you're a lifesaver."

Jilly hugged her back, surprised by the embrace. "No problem," she said. "I'm still going to need help, though. Do either of you want to volunteer?"

"I can do it," Grace replied. She knew Rebekah had neither the time, skill, nor patience to tackle a job like that, so she decided to spare her the pain of explaining that to Jilly.

"Thanks, Grace," Rebekah replied, relief flashed across her face. "I have to run. Do you need anything before I go?"

"I guess that depends on how you feel about tonight. Do you think it will be better or worse than last night?" Grace asked.

Rebekah groaned again. "Honestly, I have no idea. Last night was the first night, but today is Saturday, so it could go either way. Is Evie willing to work another night?"

"I haven't talked to her yet, but she seemed to have a lot of fun last night, so I hope so," Grace replied. "Has anyone checked Shelley's social media accounts? That might give us an idea of what to expect."

"No, but that's a good idea," Rebekah pulled out her phone and began to scroll, her frown deepening the longer she stared at it.

"Judging by the look on your face, it's not good news?" Grace raised her brow. She was certain people had a blast at the haunted hotel, but maybe she'd been wrong. The wait times had been long, and the actual run-time of the event was relatively short.

"Multiple videos went viral," Rebekah replied, looking up at Grace in horror. She began to shake her head. "We can't handle this. What are we going to do?"

They stared at each other in silence, no one knowing what to say or, more importantly, what to do.

"I'll call Mayor Allen," Grace finally said. "If anyone will know what to do, it's him."

While they waited for the mayor to show up, they busied themselves with breakfast preparations; Rebekah set the table while Jilly and Grace set food out on the buffet. Not long after, the usual breakfast crowd, which included Sasha and Andrea, began to file in. When Mayor Allen arrived, they offered him a plate and a cup of coffee, hopeful that would entice him to stay long enough to help them devise a solid plan.

Once everyone had helped themselves and were seated at the table, Rebekah explained the problem.

Mayor Allen cleared his throat. "How many people are you expecting?" he asked. His serious tone betrayed his smile.

"Well," Rebekah said nervously. "I can't know for sure, but I'm guessing at least double what was there last night."

The mayor stared straight ahead as he processed the information, his fork poised mid-air as if he couldn't quite believe what he'd heard. "Close to a thousand people were there last night," he said in disbelief. "And you think there will be at least double that tonight?"

Rebekah grimaced. "I'm afraid so."

"But how?"

"Shelley is much better at marketing than we originally thought," Rebekah explained. "The question is, what do we do now?"

"I'm not sure," he said, his brow furrowed. "We still have four nights, including tonight. Is there any way to spread these people out?"

Rebekah looked hesitant to respond. "I—"

"What about a giveaway?" Grace interrupted.

"What do you mean?" asked Rebekah. She looked relieved that someone else had joined the conversation.

"I mean, what if we offer a drawing for the next four nights and have Shelley advertise it. People could enter through her social media somehow." Grace waved her hand dismissively. "We can then divide the tickets into four and advise those in each group to only show up on the night they could win."

All eyes turned to Rebekah. "That's a lot to accomplish in a very short time," she replied. "Campaigns like you suggest usually take months to prepare, let alone run."

"But is it doable?" Mayor Allen asked.

"Maybe," Rebekah said hesitantly. She did not look convinced but appeared unwilling to say so.

"We could at least try," Jilly said, a note of hopefulness in her tone. "Unless anyone else has an idea, this is all we have."

"Thanks, guys," Grace said dryly.

"What would the giveaways consist of?" asked Rebekah. "It has to be something people actually want, and it has to be something you can put together quickly since the first giveaway will be tonight."

Grace thought about it for a minute; what did people want? "We could offer a spa package," she suggested. "Those are usually pretty popular."

"True, but that will require the winner to come back here, and they may not want to do that," Rebekah replied. "Plus, they'll have to try to work it into their schedule."

"Okay," Grace sighed. "Then what should we offer, some kind of video game console?"

"That's not a bad idea," said Jilly. "People love those. Could you get four of them on such short notice?"

"Probably not the newest ones. Would that matter?" Grace asked. She looked around the table and winced a bit. No one there was a gamer or had kids that were gamers. They were out of their depth, and they knew it.

"How about this," said Jilly. "Grace and I can run up to the city and see what we can find. We'll report back, and if it works, we'll make the purchases while Rebekah arranges the giveaway. Will that work?"

Rebekah nodded. "I need to run out to the winery this morning, but as soon as you call, I'll switch tasks. What happens if it won't work, though. Should we come up with a plan b?"

"There's no time for that," said Grace. "If it doesn't work out, we're probably hosed."

"Fair enough," said Rebekah. She stood up and gathered her things. "I'll be waiting for your call."

Grace began to clear the table, surprised that Mayor Allen was still around; she had expected him to take off as soon as they had a plan.

"You've been doing a great job, Grace," he told her. "Maybe a little too good," he smiled. "We may need to tone things down a bit from now on. The town can only handle so much."

"I agree," Grace replied. "We never expected the haunt-ed hotel event to get so out of hand," she told him. "That was also a surprise to us and not necessarily a welcome one."

Mayor Allen glanced at Jilly and then turned his attention back to Grace. "I'm glad to hear we're on the same page," he got up and prepared to leave. "I guess I'll see you ladies tonight. Good luck on your shopping trip."

Grace finished clearing the table and stacked the plates in the sink. She would have to load the dishwasher later if they wanted any chance of pulling off the impossible. "Are you ready to go?" she asked Jilly.

Jilly nodded and grabbed her purse. "The kids are with my grandma today, but I need to be back by dinner. Do you think that will be a problem?"

"I sure hope not," Grace replied. "If it is, we've got problems. Big problems."

The trip to the city took the usual forty-five minutes, though Grace tried to hurry without breaking any laws. She had never owned a video game system, so she had no idea what to look for, what was considered 'popular,' or what it would cost. On top of that, while this had been her idea, she was very concerned it would backfire. Once people heard about the giveaway, it might entice even more people to sign up, and they could end up with out-of-control crowds four nights in a row instead of something more manageable.

"You're awfully quiet," Jilly teased.

"I'm worried this is a bad idea," Grace replied. "Maybe we should offer something people won't want. I mean, the goal is to reduce the crowd, right?"

"True, but offering something people don't want might mean they don't enter the giveaway. The goal is to get them to spread out their visit, not deter them from coming. Which we can't do," she pointed out.

"Are we sure we can't deter them?" asked Grace.

"Anything you try at this point will only make people more curious," she replied. "And curiosity is the main reason they're coming."

Grace nodded. Jilly was right, which meant they needed to stay the course and hope for the best. That's all anyone can do anyway.

As predicted, the stores were sold out of the newest consoles, but they did have a cool-looking bundle, at least to Grace, of the next latest model. True gamers likely already had them, but Grace didn't expect that crowd to make up most of Shelley's followers. In fact, now that she thought about it, the people who followed Shelley might not be interested in video games at all.

She sighed as she pulled out her phone to call Rebekah. Nothing they could do about it now. "We got the consoles," she informed Rebekah when she answered the phone.

"Great!" she replied. "I'll get to work on the giveaway. Meet you back at your house around two?"

"Sounds good," Grace nodded despite Rebekah not being able to see her.

"Looks like I'll have you home in plenty of time for dinner," Grace told Jilly.

Jilly smiled as they got in the car. "I never doubted you. Let's just hope the rest of the day is uneventful."

"We can always hope," Grace smiled back.

-Days till Halloween-

Two

T he day started like any other: chores at the ranch, breakfast, cleaning, you know, the usual. It wasn't until lunch that things went sideways.

To everyone's immense relief, the giveaway had done the trick; the crowd at the previous night's haunted hotel event much more manageable. Or people had lost interest, and they were wasting time and money on a giveaway that wasn't necessary. Either way, Grace and Rebekah were just happy things had calmed down.

Once their stress level had lowered, they had even had fun. Evie, Junior, Riley, and Katie had become more and more dramatic as the night went on, each new version of the play more hilarious than the last. Multiple visitors had been seen with cameras out, so Grace hoped the group would get the props they deserved.

Shelley, who was always over-the-top dramatic, was in top form, more than earning her fair share of the profits. This was Shelley's calling. If only they had a consistent way to channel her energy and creativity into something that didn't include her risking her life for views and likes.

The fair was set to start around six; the carnival company already in town setting up. The movie-in-the-park event was over; Mike, who had been staying at the hotel, currently packing up his equipment and preparing to move on to the next location. With all the changes occurring, Grace and Rebekah felt a meeting was necessary to ensure everyone was still on the same page. They hosted a lunch barbecue to make things easier and invited everyone to attend. 'Everyone' included the town council, the actors from the Haunted Hotel event, Cole, Thorne, Emilio, Vanessa, Grant, Molly, and Sasha, and Andrea since they needed to eat, too.

Which brings us back to lunch. Once everyone was served and found a place to sit, Grace attempted to start the meeting, only to be interrupted by the doorbell. Surprised, she looked around to see if anyone was missing, but when they all appeared to be accounted for, she went to see who it could be.

Grace opened the door and found an older Hispanic couple waiting, along with a younger woman who appeared to be around Grace's age.

"Hi," Grace said politely. "Is there something I can do for you?" She assumed they were there for the wedding, but it seemed prudent to ask since she didn't know for sure.

"We're Emilio's parents," the older woman replied.

She neither looked nor sounded happy, immediately making Grace uncomfortable and concerned.

"Please, come in," Grace said, stepping back to give them room to walk around her. Once inside, she closed the door and led them to the deck in the back of the house. "We're having lunch right now, and there is more than enough for you to join us," Grace told them.

"We won't be staying long," the older woman informed Grace.

"Oh," Grace replied, unsure of what to say. She wanted to ask why, but the older woman was so unfriendly, Grace was afraid to hear her answer.

When they reached the deck, those facing the door looked up with interest at the newcomers. Emilio immediately jumped up and moved to hug his parents.

"Mom, Dad!" he exclaimed. "I'm so glad to see you. I thought you couldn't come?" he said, looking between them.

Vanessa stood up and began to cross the deck when Emilio's mom gave her a look so full of anger and disdain it stopped her in her tracks.

"We're only staying long enough for you to pack up your things and return home where you belong," Emilio's mom replied.

"Excuse me?" Emilio said, raising his brow.

"You heard me," she repeated. "This foolishness has gone on long enough, young man. It's time for you to come home where you belong."

Emilio looked around as the rest of the group looked away, trying to pretend they weren't watching. Clearly embarrassed, he tried to reason with his mother. "Why don't we take this somewhere more private," he suggested.

"There's nothing to discuss," she said. "Just pack your things, and we'll be on our way."

"No, Mom," he said defiantly, "I will not 'just pack my things,' and we will not 'be on our way'. You, however, are free to return to Texas anytime."

"Lucia," Emilio's Dad said as he took her arm. "We should go."

"Absolutely not," she said, yanking free from his grasp. "I came here to get my son, and I am not leaving without him."

"In that case," he replied. Alexia and I will leave without you. Come along," he said to the younger woman.

"But you told me Emilio wanted me back," Alexia protested. "I came all this way," she said, shaking her head.

Emilio's eyes went wide as his mouth opened in shock. "You did what?" he said to his mother. "How could you?"

Lucia lifted her chin as she faced her son. "I did what was necessary," she proclaimed. "You told me before you left Alexia was the one that got away. Well, look, she's here now, so you can come home and resume the life you had before you deserted your family."

"You need to leave," he said quietly. "Now."

Grace had never seen Emilio this angry before; in fact, she had never seen him angry at all. Since it was her house, she felt obligated to do something; she just wasn't sure what that something should be. In desperation, she glanced from Rebekah to Cole to Mayor Allen, silently begging one of them to step in. When none of them did, she sighed and walked over to the feuding family.

"We have some lovely rooms set up for you at the hotel," Grace said cheerfully. "I'm sure you would all like a chance to rest and relax after such a long drive, so why don't I take you over there so you can get settled in?" Since the dad seemed the most likely to cooperate, she focused on him, gently guiding him toward the door.

"Come along, Lucia," he said firmly.

Grace held her breath while she waited to see if Lucia would follow. When she finally, albeit reluctantly, did, Grace released her breath in relief.

"We will discuss this later," Lucia said to Emilio.

"No, we won't," Emilio replied.

Emilio watched them leave, then turned to Vanessa. "I'm so sorry," he said, taking her hands. "I don't know what's wrong with them, but it doesn't matter; the wedding will continue without them."

Tears ran down Vanessa's cheeks. "But they're your family," she whispered.

"You're my family," he replied. "My parents will either get over it, or they won't," he shrugged.

"Wait a minute," Shelley said, standing up so everyone can see her. "Did your parents just bring some woman here to convince you to leave Vanessa and return home with them?"

"Um, yes..." said Emilio. "Why?"

"Duh," Shelley said. "That's the exact skit we're doing at the hotel. That chick's not pregnant, is she?"

Emilio looked visibly uncomfortable. "I don't know, but if she is, it isn't mine."

"That's what they all say," Shelley shrugged, then sat down and went back to scrolling through her phone.

"Please ignore that," Emilio told Vanessa.

Sasha, who had remained quiet until then, approached her daughter and future son-in-law. "Why don't we go upstairs and talk?" she said quietly.

Vanessa nodded and allowed them to guide her upstairs while the rest of the guests looked around uncomfortably.

"Is there anything in particular we need to discuss," Mayor Allen asked Rebekah.

Rebekah looked up from the plate she had been staring at. "I don't know," she admitted sheepishly. "Grace had a few things to say but didn't get a chance to share them with me before you arrived."

"In that case, those of you who can should wait for Grace to return; the rest of us will have to catch up with you later," he said as he stood, readying himself to leave.

"I'm sure Grace won't be that long," Rebekah protested.

"Given the situation, I can't say I agree," Mayor Allen replied. "Regardless, I have some things I must attend to. Thank you for lunch; if Grace needs me, tell her to give me a call."

Rebekah watched helplessly as everyone got up and left, likely more from embarrassment than an actual need to leave. Grace would be disappointed to come home to an empty house, but there seemed to be little she could do to stop them.

"Don't worry about it," Cole told her. "Grace will understand. She might even be relieved."

"I suppose you're right," Rebekah replied. "Thanks for staying," she said to Cole, Thorne, and Jilly.

"We wouldn't dream of leaving you to clean this mess by yourselves, right guys?" Jilly said to Thorne and Cole.

"Right," they replied in unison.

They began clearing the table; Granny, Gladys, and Andrea excused themselves to return to their rooms. Despite

Mayor Allen's earlier prediction, Grace only took twenty minutes to return.

"How did it go?" asked Rebekah.

Grace shook her head. "Lucia hated everything, up to and including the bedspread color. Tony, Emilio's Dad, did his best to calm her, but once Alexia saw her room, she too began to complain, and at that point, there was no pleasing them, so I left."

"You just left in the middle of their complaints?" Rebekah asked, clearly impressed.

"I told them if they were unhappy with their accommodations, I could make a reservation for them at a hotel in the city," Grace replied. "When they discovered they would have to drive another forty-five minutes to get there, they changed their mind," Grace rolled her eyes.

"Hopefully they'll leave soon," said Rebekah.

"Yeah," Grace said. "Though I fear they're more likely to hang around and try to stop the wedding. Poor Emilio and Vanessa," she shook her head sadly.

Rebekah shook her head as well. "Kind of makes me glad my parents cut me off," she joked.

Grace looked at Cole, their conversation from the other day flashing through her mind. She gave him a small smile, grateful this wasn't a problem they would likely face. When he smiled back, she knew he felt the same way.

"I guess we'll just have to see how things go and do our best to deal with whatever comes our way," Grace said.

"Maybe we'll get lucky," Rebekah said hopefully.

"Maybe," Grace replied, but she doubted it after the way Lucia carried on earlier.

***

Cole and Grace walked hand-in-hand around the fair, taking in the sights as they debated which ride to go on first. They finally agreed on the Ferris Wheel and, after standing in line, sat on one of the benches.

"What are you thinking about?" asked Cole as he wrapped an arm around her shoulders and pulled her close.

"I was just wondering if we've had any families stay with us that didn't have some kind of drama or dysfunction," she replied. She snuggled close to him and laid her head on his shoulder.

The sky was clear with stars as far as the eye could see. Being there, just the two of them, she could almost forget about everything else that was going on.

"The families at Easter didn't cause any drama," Cole pointed out. "Nor did they seem dysfunctional. Julie and Journee, even though they engaged in some drama, seemed pretty normal as well."

Grace nodded as she remembered her time with the people mentioned. "You're right," she agreed. "I guess I forgot about them since Easter and Mother's Day were full of drama and problems," she said, as Dot and Valerie came to mind.

"Hey," Cole said, lifting her face to meet his. "I know you feel bad for Emilio and Vanessa. I do, too, but this isn't your problem to solve."

"I know, it's just..."

Cole kissed her as he gently caressed her face. "I love you for always wanting to help, but this is one time when you need to stay out of it. Vanessa and Emilio need to learn to stand together."

Grace reached up and cupped his cheek. His five o'clock shadow was prickly against her skin, but she loved how it added to his rugged cowboy look. "When did you become so wise?" she teased.

He shrugged. "Years of experience," he grinned. "I should warn you, my motives are not altogether altruistic."

"Oh yeah," she replied. "And why is that?"

"Tonight," he murmured against her lips. "I would prefer to have my lovely fiancé all to myself."

"I believe that can be arranged." She kissed him back, disappointed when the ride ended, and they had to get off.

They walked around a while longer, the crowds quickly growing tiresome. After one last check-in at the hotel, where they were assured everything was under control, they took off for the ranch.

"Why does it always feel like we never have enough time together," Grace asked as they walked to the door.

Cole stopped walking and turned to face her. He took her hands in his as he looked into her eyes. "I'm pretty sure I could spend every second of every day with you, and it still wouldn't feel like enough time."

Grace tugged on his hands, pulling him close to wrap her arms around his neck. "I feel the same way," she whispered.

They stood together, swaying in the moonlight to a song only they could hear, holding on to the moment for as long as they could. Tomorrow would bring a new set of problems to solve and obstacles to overcome, but tonight was for them, and they would do their best to make the most of it.

-Day till Halloween-

One

"They're gone," Grace announced when she entered the room.

Rebekah, Jilly, Granny, and Gladys stopped eating and looked up at her expectantly.

"Who's gone?" asked Granny.

"Emilio's parents," Grace replied. "When I got to the hotel, the door to their room was wide open, the bed looked like it'd never been slept in, and they were nowhere to be found. Same for Alexia's room, though hers had a few dirty towels on the floor in the bathroom."

"Do you think they went home?" asked Jilly. She looked uncertain, as if she couldn't believe they would go quietly into the night after the scene they'd created the day before.

"I have no idea," Grace shrugged. "I guess I could ask Vanessa if they know what happened. It feels a bit...intrusive, though. What do y'all think?"

They looked at each other for a moment as they considered their options.

"You do need to know if there are guests at the hotel," Rebekah pointed out. "Especially since there will be another event tonight."

Grace sighed. "I was afraid you were going to say that." She pulled out her phone and scrolled to Vanessa's number. "I'll call now."

The phone rang for so long Grace assumed no one would answer, but right before she hung up, a groggy voice came on the line.

"Hello," said Vanessa.

"Hi Vanessa, it's Grace. Did I wake you?" Grace winced, thoroughly regretting this call.

"No, we've been up all night," Vanessa replied. "Emilio's parents came by and refused to leave until he agreed to go home with them. They've been sitting on the couch for hours," she whispered. "We never should have opened the door."

Grace's eyes widened as she tried to imagine what Vanessa was going through. She was starting to think Evie had the right idea of eloping all along, though that wasn't entirely fair since her wedding to Jake had turned out beautifully.

"Is there anything I can do?" Grace asked, sure there wasn't, but feeling compelled to ask anyway. "I can bring some breakfast over," she offered.

"Breakfast might help," Vanessa said gratefully. "And coffee, please bring coffee. I made so much last night we're completely out, and I'm afraid to leave for fear they won't let me back in."

"I'll be there as soon as possible," Grace assured her. She hung up the phone and looked around. "Vanessa needs backup," Grace explained. "We need breakfast, coffee, decaf from the sound of it, and a couple of no-nonsense, take-no-prisoners type of volunteers."

"Where's Emilio in all this?" asked Jilly. "Shouldn't he be the one rescuing her? They're his parents, after all."

"I don't know where he is," said Grace. "Vanessa didn't say, and I didn't think to ask."

"Let me just say this: it will only get worse from here," Jilly said in a tone that hinted at personal experience. "I'm willing to help, but Emilio's butt needs to be kicked into action."

Granny and Gladys nodded in agreement. "Jilly's right," said Granny. "Emilio needs to step up and deal with his parents. If he can't or won't, I'm afraid Vanessa needs to take this for the sign it is and leave while she still can."

"Okay, new plan," said Grace. "Instead of 'Operation Save Vanessa,' it is now 'Operation Find Emilio and kick his butt into gear.'"

"I'll get behind that," Rebekah volunteered.

"Thanks, give me a few minutes, and I'll be ready to go," said Grace. She put together several large containers of pastries, muffins, and breakfast burritos, added a bag of coffee grounds, and threw in a stack of napkins and plastic silverware for good measure. Once that was done, she returned to the dining room. "Okay, I'm ready," she announced.

Rebekah and Jilly stood up and grabbed their things. "We're right behind you," said Jilly.

Once outside, they piled into Grace's car, Rebekah in the passenger seat and Jilly in the back. Vanessa and Emilio lived in Hope Springs, a town about twice the size of Winterwood located thirty minutes west of them. Before she headed in that direction, she decided to run by Emilio's office, just in case. Grace didn't want to believe Emilio would abandon Vanessa but had a feeling he might do so using work as an excuse. Unfortunately, she appeared to be correct, as Emilio's car was parked in front of the building.

Sighing, she parked beside him and got out, the other two following close behind. "I wasn't sure about the butt-kicking part before, but I'm definitely on board now," said Grace.

"Oh yeah," said Jilly. "He has it coming.

They walked into the office, three determined women on a mission. One look at their faces, and Emilio was on his feet, hands up in submission as he backed up toward the wall.

"I had a client meeting I couldn't miss," he said quickly. "I had no choice but to come to work, I swear."

All three of them crossed their arms and glared at him.

"And you couldn't have kicked your parents out *before* you left for the office?" Jilly asked.

"Why allow them inside in the first place?" asked Rebekah. "They made their position more than clear at the barbecue."

"I was hoping they had come to apologize," he said sadly. "It wasn't until they were inside, I realized how wrong I was to hope for that."

"And?" Jilly raised her brow.

"And what?" he asked, confused. "They refused to leave. What was I supposed to do?"

"Kick them out," Jilly said, exasperated. "If they still refuse, call the police. You're only a victim if you choose to be," she reminded him.

Emilio ran his hand through his hair. "You want me to call the police on my parents?" he asked. He looked shocked.

"Not really," Jilly replied. "Usually, just the threat is enough to get people moving. You have to do something, though. You can't just allow them to terrorize your fiance indefinitely, and you especially can't do that while you hide out here like a coward."

Emilio looked down in shame. "You're right," he said quietly.

"Yes, I am," Jilly said, her tone gentler than before. "I know they're your parents, Emilio. If you can't stand up to them for whatever reason, that's okay, but if that's the case, you must let Vanessa go. She doesn't deserve this."

"There are cultural differences you're unaware of," he said defensively.

"I acknowledged that," Jilly reminded him. "But those differences aren't going to change, and only you can decide if you can overcome them."

"It's not about me; it's about them," he said in frustration. "They have to decide to overcome them, not me."

"Look," Jilly said, her voice firm. "I'm willing to admit there are things I don't understand, but that doesn't change the facts. Are you willing to marry Vanessa if your parents refuse to accept her? Because if not, you need to end this now."

"You need to end this regardless," said Rebekah, her arms still crossed. "The wedding is supposed to be tomorrow, and there are still a thousand things to do. We do not have time for this."

Emilio sank into his desk chair. "I'll take care of it," he muttered.

Grace could see how dejected he looked and decided to take pity on him. "I have some food for you in the car," she told him. It may help calm things down a little when you get home.

"Thanks, Grace," he said. "I appreciate it, and I know Vanessa will, too. I'll let you know what happened later today."

She nodded, then motioned to Rebekah and Jilly. They had done what they could; the rest was up to him. Unfortunately, the outcome would be bittersweet unless his parents changed their minds. Someone was going to get their heart broken, which seemed...wrong. Weddings were supposed to bring people together, not tear families apart.

***

Not knowing what else to do and needing something to fill the time, Grace and Jilly spent the day working on the cake. They figured plenty of people would need a pick-me-up if the wedding were canceled, and what better pick-me-up than a large, three-tier, custom-made cake?

Grace had never been ambitious enough to make anything more than a single-layer sheet cake, so this had been an experience, one she was glad to share with her new friend. Since the inside of the cake was up to them, they decided to go all out, as much as possible in two days, and make a surprise spill cake with Halloween-themed sprinkles and candy. Jilly had shown Grace a couple of videos of people cutting one of those open, and Grace immediately agreed to do one. It would be so cool; she just hoped Emilio and Vanessa would be the ones to do the 'spilling.'

They had just finished the crumb coat when Emilio and Vanessa walked in, glum expressions on their faces.

"They're gone," Emilio announced.

"Is the wedding off?" asked Grace cautiously.

Emilio shook his head. "No, the wedding is still on; my parents just won't be attending."

"What happened," Jilly asked gently.

"I did what you said," he replied. "I told them I was marrying Vanessa whether they liked it or not, and if they refused to support me and my new wife, there was no room for them in my life."

Vanessa took his hand and gazed sadly at his face. "I tried to reason with them," she said sadly. "But they were adamant I'd stolen their son, and there was nothing I could say to change their minds."

"Out of curiosity," Grace said sheepishly. "What was the deal with Alexia?"

"She was my high school girlfriend," Emilio explained. "We broke up right before college since we were attending different ones. I haven't seen her since, so I have no idea why my parents thought I would choose her over Vanessa. It's been at least ten years," he said, his brow furrowed in confusion.

"I'm curious why she agreed to their plan," said Grace.

"From what I gathered," said Vanessa. "The degree she chose didn't net the career, or more importantly, the salary she'd hoped for, and she's drowning in student loans. His parents told her about Emilio's new job and promised he would take care of her."

Emilio gave her a strange look. "They said all that in front of you?" he asked in surprise.

"They didn't know I speak Spanish," she said sheepishly.

"And you conveniently forgot to tell them," Jilly laughed.

Vanessa shrugged. "It's not my fault they made incorrect assumptions."

Grace took a deep breath and let it out slowly. "I'm sorry," she told Emilio. "I'm happy you and Vanessa are going through with the wedding. I just wish the circumstances were different."

"I appreciate that," he replied. "It's okay, though. As long as the person who matters most is there, I'll be happy." He smiled at Vanessa, his love for her clear to everyone.

"I take it no one else has shown up?" Vanessa asked, her eyes never leaving Emilio's.

Grace shook her head. "I'm sorry, but no. But the whole town plans to be there, so I doubt you'll find a single empty seat!" Grace said enthusiastically.

"That's very sweet of you to say," Vanessa told her. "You've all worked so hard. I'm sure it will be the wedding of our dreams, even without extended friends and family members."

"We'll make sure of it," Grace assured her.

They said their goodbyes. Emilio and Vanessa were too worn out to face the dinner crowd. Grace had volunteered to let Vanessa stay in one of the extra guestrooms, but she had politely declined, claiming to want to be alone with Emilio instead. After the night they'd had, Grace couldn't blame her; she just hoped the festive mood would return by tomorrow night. No one wanted to get married in a state of gloom and doom.

Happy Halloween

"Happy Halloween!" Grace exclaimed excitedly once everyone had gathered at the breakfast table.

"Happy Halloween!" they shouted in unison.

Grace grinned at her friends and family, excited to share such a fun holiday. She then turned her attention to Granny. "Do I finally get to see my costume?" she asked. She batted her eyelashes at Granny. "Pretty please," she begged.

Granny laughed. "It's supposed to be a surprise," she teased. "You can see when it's time to get ready for the wedding."

"Ugh, fine," Grace replied. "But I was hoping to wear it all day. Halloween only comes around once a year, you know."

"True," Granny replied. "But you still have a lot to do before it's time for the wedding. You don't want to ruin your costume before everyone has a chance to see it."

Rebekah laughed. "You sound like a little kid," she teased Grace.

"I feel like a little kid," Grace replied. "Aren't you dying to see the costume they made you?"

"Of course," Rebekah replied. "But unlike you, I am a patient person."

Grace raised her brow.

"Okay, fine," Rebekah relented. "They already told me no when I asked earlier!"

They laughed, for once free of stress and worry. Grace couldn't help but notice how nice it was to have a meal together without discussing business. She looked forward to Thanksgiving, where they would have a proper holiday meal, just their immediate friends and family, though at this point, Grace considered them more family than friends.

Rebekah, Molly, Grant, Gladys, Granny, Cole, Riley, and Thorne sat with her at the table. There would be a few extras at Thanksgiving, and she would gladly welcome them, but the ones with her now were the ones that mattered most. Especially the handsome cowboy seated to her left.

Their happy mood was shattered by a wail as Vanessa rushed into the room, a tattered black dress in her hands, tears streaming down her cheeks. "It's ruined," she sobbed. "My wedding dress is ruined."

Grace looked at Rebekah, then rushed to Vanessa's side. "Here, let me," she said, gently prying the dress from Vanessa's hands. She walked it over to Granny and held it up for her to see. "Can you fix it?" she asked Granny hopefully.

Granny and Gladys gave it a once over, then gave each other a look.

"Call Jilly and ask her to come over," Granny replied slowly. "I can't make any promises, but between the three of us, we might be able to do something."

Vanessa looked up with a hopeful expression on her face. "Really?" she asked. "You think you can fix it?"

Granny hesitated to respond. "We're going to try, dear."

Grace pulled out her phone and sent an emergency text to Jilly, who quickly texted that she'd be there in five minutes. In the meantime, Grace helped Granny and Gladys to Granny's room and set them up at their sewing machines. There was no doubt in her mind they would either fix the dress or come up with something entirely different but just as good. The thought got her excited about her own wedding dress, but she quickly pushed those thoughts out of her mind. This wasn't the time for daydreaming.

When Jilly arrived, she went straight to Granny's room, barely waving hello on her way through the dining room. While they waited for the verdict, Grace asked Vanessa what happened to the dress.

"I was so excited when I got up this morning, I went to try on the dress; that's when I discovered it'd been ruined," she explained.

Grace exchanged looks with Rebekah. You didn't have to be an ace detective to figure out who the likely culprit was, which was sad. This was one more hurdle Emilio's parents would have to overcome if they ever decided to mend fences with their son. Grace didn't envy that task, though she hoped they would try one day.

As they waited, the group began to disperse. Molly and Grant were the first to leave, little Eliza needing to be fed and changed. Next went Rebekah and Thorne, each needing to go to work, then Riley, who had a few chores to tend to before the wedding later that day. That left Cole, Grace, and Vanessa, the latter still distraught.

"This wedding has been cursed since the second I found out I'd won," Vanessa said, her eyes staring straight ahead, her tone empty and hollow. "I should have never entered that contest."

Grace reached across the table and placed her hand on Vanessa's. "Don't say things like that," Grace said gently. "All weddings are stressful. Remember Evie's? They had all kinds of problems, but look at her and Jake now; both of them are happy as can be."

"Grace is right," said Cole. "Nothing ever goes off without a hitch, especially things worth having."

Their earlier conversation with Emilio popped into her head. Emilio had claimed things had been interesting lately and expected them to return to normal after the wedding. Grace now wondered if more had been going on than they knew about. She was about to ask when Jilly peaked her head out of Granny's room and called for Vanessa.

"Should we be concerned?" Grace asked Cole once Vanessa was safely out of earshot.

"I'm not sure," he replied. "I understand why she's upset, but it feels like there's more to it than what's on the surface. Although, what's on the surface is more than enough to be upset about."

"I agree," Grace nodded.

Before long, Vanessa came running out of the room, tears streaming down her face. Without pausing to say goodbye, she hurried through the dining room and out the front door, leaving Grace and Cole stunned.

"I take it you couldn't fix the dress?" Grace asked Jilly when she appeared a few minutes later.

Jilly grinned. "Actually, it's better than it was before. As soon as she looked in the mirror, Vanessa burst into tears, I'm assuming from happiness."

That was not how it looked to Grace, but what did she know? She'd heard of brides getting emotional on their wedding day, so maybe that's all it was.

***

It was finally time for Grace, Rebekah, and Molly to see their costumes. Grace felt like a little kid on Christmas morning, finally seeing what Santa brought.

They filed into Granny's room and took a seat on the bed.

"Molly," said Gladys. "You can go first," she said, holding a Princess Peach costume. "And here's one for little Eliza," Gladys said, handing her a tiny peach costume.

"Oh my gosh," Molly said, putting her hand over her mouth. "It's a little peach," she said, showing Grace and Rebekah a costume resembling the fruit. "If only I could get Grant to dress up like Mario," Molly laughed.

"You mean like this?" Grant said as he appeared dressed like Mario.

Molly's eyes went wide in shock. "In all the years we've been together, you've never once worn a costume," she exclaimed.

"Times change," Grant shrugged. "I can't let my girls go out all dressed up without me."

"Thank you so much," Molly said to Gladys before getting up and hugging Grant. "If you're not careful, Eliza may end up with a little brother or sister," she teased him.

They left the room together, and Grace could hear them laughing at something as she patiently waited her turn.

"Okay," said Gladys. "Now it's time for Rebekah's costume," she said, pulling out a long, flowing dress with a colorful flower pattern.

"It's a hippie costume," Rebekah said excitedly. "This is so cool, and I have just the boots and jewelry to wear with it."

"Don't forget your hairband," said Granny, handing her a matching hairband.

"Or your hippie boyfriend," said Thorne.

Their mouths dropped open when Thorne walked in looking like he'd stepped straight out of a sixties Woodstock photo, round John Lennon glasses and all. Now Molly's laughter made sense, and Grace couldn't help but pull out her phone and take a picture.

Rebekah and Thorne left, presumably so Rebekah could change and get over to the winery. She still had a few last-minute details to see to before the wedding began and needed to get there before everyone else.

"Now, can I see my costume?" Grace asked, trying hard not to sound impatient.

Granny smiled and pulled a costume out of her closet. "I suppose I've kept you waiting long enough," she said. She handed Grace a gorgeous medieval-style black dress trimmed in green and a black cape with a velvet green underlining.

"It's gorgeous!" Grace exclaimed, holding the costume to her chest. It was so beautiful she was disappointed she would only get to wear it for one night. It may be time to bring capes back into fashion.

"It's a witch costume," said Granny, handing Grace a crystal ball.

"And I am your dashing and debonair vampire fiance," said Cole.

Grace turned to stare at Cole, silently taking in the sight of his fake teeth, elegant all-black suit, black cape with blood-red lining, pale skin, and slicked-back hair. Dashing and debonair did not do him justice. If she thought he was sexy in his usual cowboy attire, which she did, he was drop-dead gorgeous in his suit and cape.

He held out his hand, and, mesmerized, she reached for it without thought. It's a good thing he isn't really a vampire, or she would be in trouble, though she doubted she would mind.

"Thank you so much," Grace told Granny. She let go of Cole long enough to hug her grandmother, then returned to his side. "I'll be back to help you two in a few minutes," Grace assured them.

"Take your time, dear," said Granny. "Gladys and I are going to sit this one out."

"Are you sure?" Grace asked, concerned they would choose to miss such a big occasion.

"We're sure," said Granny. "Gladys and I are going to hang out on the porch and hand out candy to the youn-guns'," she said happily.

Grace remembered all those years they had been unable to afford Halloween candy and instantly knew how important this was to Granny. She gave Granny another hug. "I understand," she whispered.

She took Cole's hand and left the room with him, anxious to try on her costume. Once she was dressed, with Rebekah's help, she went back downstairs and into his waiting arms. "I'm not sure I'd mind missing the wedding myself," she teased, staring into his deep blue eyes.

"I wouldn't either," he said thoughtfully. "But alas, I cannot deprive the world of seeing how beautiful you look in your costume."

Grace laughed and followed him to his truck. Going to an event she wasn't responsible for was nice; it was definitely something she could get used to. When they arrived at the winery, she looked around in surprise. She had expected Emilio and Vanessa's wedding to resemble Evie and Jake's, with a Halloween-themed twist. It did, except there were at least half a dozen media outlets there, including one that represented the radio station.

A little self-conscious at being seen on camera, she clung tightly to Cole's arm and allowed him to lead them around as she gawked at Rebekah's handiwork. Rebekah had really outdone herself. Tasteful decorations lined the walkways, purple twinkle lights were strung in the trees and across the yard, and purple and black roses intertwined with lights to form table centerpieces.

Cole and Grace sat at a table with Evie, Jake, Molly, Grant, Riley, Katie, Thorne, and Jilly. Evie and Jake were dressed as Gomez and Morticia Addams, Jilly was Little Bo Peep, and Katie and Riley were Fred and Daphne from Scooby Doo.

Grace looked around for Sasha and Andrea. They had left before she could see their costumes, and Grace was curious to see what they decided. She spotted them at a table near the front of the tent: Andrea in a Glinda the Good Witch costume, Sasha dressed as a nineteen-forties flapper girl. Grace's suggestion to check out the vintage store had paid off.

Similar to Evie and Jake's wedding, tents containing the tables lined up in front of the pier. A walkway made of dark, glowing stones wove from the back of the tents up to the edge of the pier, where Emilio, dressed as Frankenstein's monster, waited with Pastor Allen.

Not long after Cole and Grace took their seats, an instrumental version of 'This is Halloween' from 'The Nightmare Before Christmas' began to play as Vanessa slowly made her way down the path, steam rising from the glowing stones as she walked. She was dressed as the Bride of Frankenstein, her hair and makeup flawless, her dress the envy of every costume designer. The special effects gave the wedding a movie-like feel, the assorted cameramen and women filming from the sides adding to the effect.

As soon as Vanessa finished her progression and joined Emilio at the altar, which was comprised of a wooden arch painted black and lined with purple and black roses, Pastor Allen began the ceremony.

When he asked if anyone objected to the marriage, Grace held her breath, then released it slowly when no one spoke up. Pastor Allan was about to continue when a scream broke the silence, followed by the sight of a woman running across the lawn, a man close behind her.

The wedding guests watched in stunned silence as the two bypassed the tents and ran straight for the couple at the altar.

"I object," the woman said. She bent over at the waist and placed her hands on her knees as she panted, out of breath from her fast-paced trek across the winery.

"No, she doesn't," said the man.

Grace immediately recognized them as Emilio's parents and wondered once more how people kept getting past security. She could only watch helplessly as the scene unfolded before them, the cameras capturing every horrible second and forever immortalizing it for the world to see.

"Yes, I do," Lucia argued. She opened her mouth to say more, but Vanessa cut her off.

"I'm pregnant," she blurted out. She turned to Emilio, who appeared to be in shock, but his monster makeup made it hard to tell. "I was going to tell you after the wedding," she explained.

"How long have you known?" he asked.

"About a month," Vanessa replied warily. "When I found out I'd won the free wedding package, I thought it was a sign we were meant to be a family. I would have told you sooner, but I didn't want you to feel trapped and forced to go through with the wedding."

"I'm going to be a grandma?" asked Lucia. Her hands were to her mouth, making it hard to hear her, but there was no mistaking the sudden change in her demeanor.

"I'm going to be a father," Emilio echoed.

"Ahem," Pastor Allen cut in. "Should we continue, or would you prefer to postpone this to a later date?"

"Please, continue," said Lucia. She looked around for a couple of free chairs, and when a few appeared, no doubt thanks to Wyatt, the owner of the winery, she surprised everyone by dragging her equally stunned husband over to them and willfully taking a seat.

"We don't have to," Vanessa said quietly. "If you need some time..."

Emilio shook his head, took her hand, and turned to Pastor Allen. "Please, continue."

The rest of the ceremony went off without a hitch. Emilio and Vanessa had written their own vows, which were just as unique and creative as they were. By the time they were announced husband and wife, Grace had tears in her eyes. She just wished the cameras hadn't been present for the first part. She'd seen enough to know that scandal sells and knew the media would make the objection and secret pregnancy announcement the objects of their focus.

After the ceremony, various Halloween songs began to play over the loudspeaker as people paired off and began to dance. At one point, Grace spotted Jilly and Mayor Allen dancing, and from what she could see, they were having a great time together, laughing as they tried to do the Thriller dance.

When it was time to cut the cake, Jilly and Grace held hands as they waited for their surprise to be discovered. Judging by the shrieks of laughter from the bride and groom, their surprise was a hit, and for once, Grace was glad to see the moment captured on camera. She would make sure Jilly got the credit since she was responsible for most of the work.

Since they still had to deal with the last night of the fair and the Haunted Hotel event, Grace, Cole, and the rest of their group had to leave early. As Grace hugged Vanessa goodbye, she was surprised by her cryptic statement.

"Thank you so much for everything," Vanessa said, tears in her eyes. "I don't deserve it, but I do appreciate it."

"What do you mean?" asked Grace, her brow raised.

"Nothing," Vanessa shook her head. "Rebekah's waving me over, thanks again."

Grace watched her go. She was tempted to follow, but Cole was waiting, and they needed to go.

"Everything okay?" he asked, taking her hand in his.

She shrugged. "It is now."

They walked to the truck silently, Grace doing her best not to trip over the gravel in her high heels. Why did holidays always have to end so quickly? There was always so much planning and excitement leading up to the big day, and then, bam, it was over in the blink of an eye.

The drive to town was uneventful, Grace doing her best to take in all the costumes and decorations as they passed by. It would be time to pull out the Christmas decorations in just a few weeks.

"What about a Christmas Eve wedding?" she asked Cole.

"I thought you didn't want to get married at Christmas?"

"I've changed my mind. It is the most wonderful time of the year, you know!" She could imagine getting married among all the twinkling lights, snowflakes, and trees. It would be magical.

Cole glanced at her as he drove. "Sounds good to me," he grinned.

"Then it's settled," she said. "We can tell Granny when we get home; she'll be so excited."

Last Christmas, she'd felt like her whole world was ending; now, it felt like it was just beginning.

Afterword

Dear Reader,

Thank you so much for reading Countdown to Halloween! I had so much fun writing this book, and I sincerely hope you had fun reading it! These characters have begun to feel like family, and I love checking in with them and seeing the changes in their lives.

It was especially meaningful to take Molly and Grant from the brink of divorce last Christmas to the birth of their new daughter. In each of my books, I try to explore some of the more 'difficult' aspects of families and relationships, often focusing on forgiveness and redemption where possible. In this book it was acceptance. Sometimes there are things we can't change so we must do our best to move forward, even when it's hard.

If you'd like to stay in touch, visit my website at: www.diannahoux.com and click on Lessons from a Jilted Bride. Not only will you receive a free copy of my book, which contains Evie and Jake's story, but you'll get weekly updates, sneak peeks, access to giveaways, freebies and more!

Happy Reading!

-Dianna

About the Author

Dianna is a wife, mother, reader, writer, and small-town girl at heart. She resides in a rural Missouri town of less than twenty-five hundred people with her husband and three boys in a late 1800s home they've been lovingly restoring when she isn't busy working on her next book.

A romantic at heart, she believes in happily-ever-afters rooted in realism and, most importantly, humor!

She is the author of Forsaking the Dark, a paranormal romance, The Queen's Revenge, a historical romance, and the Holiday Countdown Series, a sweet, small-town romance series.

Acknowledgements

I would like to take a moment to give my heartfelt thanks to the following awesome people who helped to name the hotel and Bed and Breakfast. Without their help, I would likely still be staring at a blank screen and questioning my life choices!

Thank you so much:
Sasha Harrinanan
Andrea Stoeckel
Gail Pollack
Mike Pollack
Roger Jephcote
Carolyn Overcash
Shari Hamble
Barb Gary
Rebecca Torres

Made in United States
North Haven, CT
31 August 2024

56803361R00114